Jillian in the Borderlands

Beth Alvarado
October 20, 2020

Jillian in the Borderlands

a cycle of rather dark tales

Beth Alvarado

Black
Lawrence
Press

Black
Lawrence
Press

www.blacklawrence.com

Executive Editor: Diane Goettel
Cover Design: Zoe Norvell
Cover Art: "Joy Comes" by Kimi Eisele
Book Design: Amy Freels

Copyright © Beth Alvarado 2020
ISBN: 978-1-62557-821-1

Published 2020 by Black Lawrence Press.
Printed in the United States.

For Maurilio Miguel Alvarado,
who was orphaned long before he ever reached the border,
and
for all of the children who have been separated
from their parents since.

"Do you believe," said Candide, "that men have always massacred each other as they do to-day, that they have always been liars, cheats, traitors, ingrates, brigands, idiots, thieves, scoundrels, gluttons, drunkards, misers, envious, ambitious, bloody-minded, calumniators, debauchees, fanatics, hypocrites, and fools?"

—Voltaire

Jillian in the Borderlands
a cycle of rather dark tales

Tale (tāl) *n.* [ME < OE *talu*] **1.** A recital of events; a report or revelation. **2.** A story or narrative, true or fictitious, drawn up so as to interest or amuse, or to preserve the history of a fact or incident. **3.** Things told so as to violate confidence or secrecy; reports of private matters not proper to be divulged; idle or mischievous gossip. **4.** *Archaic:* a tally or reckoning.

The Dead Child Bride

*In which Jillian encounters the dead child bride and is thus
saved from the clutches of her neighbor, Mr. Wiley.*

1

Angie O'Malley stood on her porch with her daughter and watched
as Wiley drove up. This was in the desert, a thorny landscape of
hallucinatory heat where the prickly pear drill their spines into the
caliche and hope for rain, where immigrants from regions south
seek refuge and snowbirds sunshine, where bureaucrats ban books
and brown skin and birth control, where companies design sleek
missiles and pour solvents into the soil, where on streets lined with
small stucco houses cowboys shoot their guns in noisy celebration
on the Fourth of July, and where the bodies of dead girls are sometimes abandoned in alleys. Once only the arms were found; once a
seven-year-old was knocked off her bicycle and abducted; once a
two-year-old was stolen through the window of her bedroom. Such
was the climate and the atmosphere.

Angie had heard that Wiley was just a workingman. He had pulled
himself up by his bootstraps from a dusty dot in Texas to this small
plot of lawn circled by chain link. Here he could hunt to his heart's
delight and had once followed a deer all the way into Mexico, going
against human traffic, avoiding the Minutemen, stepping over the

invisible borderline, until the deer, next to a small lake, had stopped
and tilted its head to taste the wind. It was an oasis, really, tall trees
and dappled sunlight. Birdsong. No wonder the deer was so calm,
protected as it thought it was by international law. But Wiley took aim
and then, afterwards, he shouldered that carcass and slunk back across
the line. If anyone stopped him, he would just say *you can't cross what
you can't see*. At least that was his story. And he was going to stick by it.

When Wiley pulled his truck into his driveway, he tipped his cowboy hat in Angie's general direction, and said, "How's your daddy,"
which she thought odd, since her father had been dead for years, but
then she remembered Wiley was a Texan and they had unique ways
of speaking there. When he said "daddy," maybe he meant her ex-
husband, Bobby. Or maybe he was talking to her daughter, Jillian, but
everyone on the block knew Jillian couldn't talk. It suddenly occurred
to Angie that it would be just like him to set his sights on Jilli, even
though she was still just a girl. Hadn't he romanced his own seventeen-
year-old son's fourteen-year-old girlfriend? Hadn't he married her?

Angie had heard these stories from Mac, her across-the-street
neighbor, who appeared on the front porch daily with tales of woe.
Yes, Mac was the neighborhood collector of sorrows. In another
country, in another century, she would have been a professional
wailer, but here and now she was just a snoop and a dispenser of
advice no one wanted to hear.

Angie watched, her arms folded, as Wiley stepped into his house
and then, only moments later, back out. He was wearing his cowboy boots and a pair of Speedos. He threw the head of a dead deer
into the yard for his dogs to gnaw on and began to mow his grass.
Clouds, like large dark turnips, rose in the sky.

2

Angie and her sister and me, we're sitting at her kitchen table. It is
hot, as in h-o-t, hot. Sunlight melting like butter down the sliding

glass door. What with only a swamp cooler and it being July, it's probably muggier inside than out there under the mulberry trees where the kids are. I'm keeping my eye on Jillian—she's been known to pinch. Not that I haven't taught my own kids to fight back. Whatever. It's that kind of world. Anyways, Angie and Glenda and me, we're talking about May-December romances because Glenda's husband Steve has just run off with a student in his first period geometry class. Glenda's thinking about calling the girl's parents and the principal, the school board, and the newspaper.

"Add the police to the list," Angie says, and turns to me. "Don't you think so, Mac? And the TV news and *America's Most Wanted!*"

Not one to take sides, I shrug.

"He wrote me a letter," Glenda says. "On ordinary notebook paper. Just torn out of a notebook. In pencil."

How sad is that?

I remind them how Wiley, next door, he'd done the same thing. "But," I say, "I'm not sure you can call it a May-December romance if the guy's over forty and the girl a teenager. Plus the girl had first been his son's girlfriend and he had stolen her away."

"Steve thinks they're soul mates," Glenda sighs. "That's what he wrote."

"Soul mates? Now he's going to have cell mates," Angie says, and we all laugh although I can tell Glenda's hurting. She finishes off that Chablis like it's soda pop.

"He left it right there on the kitchen counter. Where Stevie Jr. could have found it." Glenda lights a cigarette. "But, you know," she makes her eyes all squinty, "I can't remember what I did with it."

"Burn it," Angie says, then changes her mind. "Give it to the cops."

"No, save it for later," I say. "A little bit of guilt can go a long way."

I tell them how Wiley first allowed the girl to move in with his son, but the parents showed up and dragged her out of there by the hair, all kinds of drama, including broken windows. And then a few days later, Wiley married her! "Of course, that night we could hear the fighting and yelling. Wiley was beating his son up, saying, *this hurts me more than it hurts you.* And, *why do you make me do this?* And, *you ungrateful little bastard.* In the morning, when the kid moved out, he had a black eye."

Angie looks at her sister. "What do you do with a dad like that?" Glenda shrugs. "I haven't told Stevie Jr. anything yet."

We look at her. We look at one another. She's taking this pretty hard.

"When do you think he started sleeping with the girl?" Angie asks—about Wiley, I guess. Not Steve.

"¿Quien sabe?" I say.

Angie gets up to open another bottle. It's past five, the shadows growing longer. Soon it'll be time to feed the kids.

"And only a few days later, she set fire to the inside of his house," I say. "Almost gutted it."

"In the letter, he included a list of my sins." Glenda sighs out a lungful of smoke. "But what were they?"

"Sins!" I refill her glass and mine. "*Eff him.*"

"I heard Wiley had the girl committed," Angie says. She takes a long look out the sliding glass door to make sure the kids aren't being mean to one another, as they will be when left to their own devices, especially if one of them is different. "What was his son's name?"

"Johnny? Ronnie? Tommy?" I say. "Whatever. He has blond hair to his shoulders." I look with meaning at Glenda. "A nice looking kid, really, if you go for the young ones."

"Hmm," Glenda smiles.

"Tit for tat, I always say."

"Make sure he's legal," Angie says.

We raise our glasses and the blood orange that is the sun gets caught there.

3

When Angie allowed herself to think about her ex-husband at all, she felt that Bobby Guzmán had deserted her for no good reason other than, as he would say, she was pinche. Most of the time she didn't miss him and she was perfectly capable of taking care of herself, thank you, but deserted in this god-forsaken desert, that's how she often felt. Marooned among morons. Mac and Wiley were the least of it. The guy on the other side had a mean Doberman and whenever the dog got out of the yard, everyone would drop what they were doing and scurry into their houses, hiding, until the damn dog was re-captured. The guys down the street from the trailer park, why, they did their own paltry versions of home invasions, waving guns around until you handed over twenty bucks or whatever. After a few years of this, no one had much left to steal. An air raid alarm, that's actually what was needed, some sort of warning *the meth-heads are coming, the meth-heads are coming* so you could stash your TV or stereo in the closet, hide the family jewels if you had any. Really, they didn't want trouble; they just wanted enough for the next fix. It was almost like a donation to keep the peace. Who worried about missiles—although they did indeed live in a town ringed by missiles—with neighbors like these?

When Angie and Bobby had found the place, it hadn't seemed as if they were surrounded by outlaws. In fact, the neighbors, like Mac and her husband, who trimmed their square green lawns every Saturday morning and washed their old cars until they gleamed, had greeted them, glad that the house, the blight of the block, had been sold. Sure the house had holes punched in the drywall and black mold in between the tiles of the showers—such was their price range—but it had been neglected by its owners and perhaps trashed by them on their way out. Nothing that soap and water and paint and hard work couldn't fix. Angie had stripped all the bright orange paint off of the cupboards in the kitchen and Bobby had stained them a warm walnut. They'd ripped up the old carpeting and layers of linoleum and he'd painted the concrete floors brick red, like those in the houses of his youth. They'd replaced the drywall and the tiles in the bathrooms. They'd built an arbor in the back yard and planted grape vines and a vegetable garden beneath it. Angie had made curtains and quilts and towels on the ancient black Singer her mother had given her.

During all of this, she had been pregnant with Jillian and she sometimes wondered if it hadn't been the chemicals that made Jilli mute, although the doctors repeatedly told her there was no rhyme or reason. Little did she know that Jillian, swimming in the warm amniotic fluid, had known everything she needed to know even then: had foreseen that in five years her father would witness the deaths of his fellow workers, one literally felled by a falling saguaro— they weighed tons, evidently—another while trimming a palm tree. Foresaw that his friend would climb up the trunk with spikes on his shoes and a belt around his waist fastening him to the tree; foresaw, also, that the dead fronds from above would come crashing down, forcing his head forward against his chest until he could no longer breathe; and foresaw, finally, that her father would not be able to get to him, no ladder would be long enough, not the extension ladder from the job, not even the ladder of the first fire truck, which would take a half an hour to arrive. Her father would have to listen to his friend cry that he did not want to die until, in fact, he did die. Her father would then sink into a deep depression, feeling that even nature was becoming malevolent, feeling there was nothing a man could do to keep his family safe. He had, after all, been helpless in the face of death. In response, he would grow his hair out and his beard and he would begin to partake, a little too much, of the beer.

Of course, none of this happened until Jillian was five. Up until then, the three of them had lived in their little house and cultivated their garden and cooked out on summer evenings, only having to hide from the bullets of their neighbors when they rained down from the heavens on the Fourth of July or New Year's Eve. It was only after these deaths he could not prevent that Jillian's father would begin to look like a sad, dark Jesus, that the neighborhood would be taken over by people who were ruled by their baser appetites, that nature would start reasserting itself—even the vines would begin growing into the house between the windows and the bricks, even the rain would drip through the roof into pots, even the waters from the rains would rise and flood in under the front door in the winter, even the winds would uproot the trees in the backyard, the trees knocking over the wall so that the lizards and rabbits and snakes and quail could come into the yard and eat from the garden, even the weeds would push their way up through the asphalt in the streets and the cracks in the sidewalks.

But since Jillian had foreseen all of this from the womb, nothing surprised her. She decided that if there was nothing her father could do, there was nothing she could say. Only her mother could see none of the signs, not of her husband's sadness, nor of the crumbling world around her. She was determined, Angie was. She was determined that, despite all evidence to the contrary, she could make of this the best of all possible worlds. Everything could be made anew and safe for Jillian. All it took was a strong will.

4

"Jilli. Jilli Bean. Wouldn't you like an itty bit more lunch, sweetie? I made you those frogs on a log you love so much." Jillian turned off the volume on *One Thousand and Three Horrible Ways to Die*, a show she was never supposed to watch. She hated it when her mother called her Jilli and she hated it when she talked to her like she was a baby. Mom, I'm not *stupid*, I'm *speechless*. That's what she would have said except for she was speechless.

Why was I born now? she'd intuited to her Maker on that fateful day of her birth, why not in the Good Old Days when she could've churned her own butter and milked the cows, although not in that order, and then gone out into the wilds with her handsome hunk of a husband who looked like Clint Eastwood when he was Rowdy Yates on that old Netflix show, when she could have been abducted by an even handsomer—if you went in for the ambiguous ethnic type, which she did, since she was one herself—Indian played by an Italian, a renegade who would ravish her as much as she wanted to be ravished and then when her husband rescued her, he wouldn't even care because, *hello,* she'd been ravished and he would love that little half-breed baby just as much as his own tow-heads.

Why now, why in this day and age, she'd wanted to ask, while the mists of heaven were still in her eyes and so for an infinitesimal split-second she could see ahead to the next day when, on her way home from school, she would encounter Wiley next door, well-named because he was so wily, as in Wile E. Coyote, and not a hunk, not by any stretch of the imagination, ethnic or otherwise. She'd seen ahead to the deer's head in the yard—this is why she would stop and look. The deer's head. It was a portent. And she knew she would look into its eyes and see alarm there and then the deer would say to her, so clearly, "Do not go into that house, Chick-a-dee. Wile E. is one sick puppy."

But at that moment, her split seconds of omniscience would end and, like the rest of us, she'd be left in suspense. What did the vision mean? Was it a warning, telling her not to go into the house, telling her she could alter her fate? Or was it simply a sign that she was fated to go into the house?

"Curiosity," the Deer's Head would tell her, "curiosity is what killed the cat."

Not one to ignore a talking Deer's Head but sure of her own agency, Jillian crept up to the sliding glass door and peered in. There she saw the Child Bride zipping around the kitchen, running her hands through the plates and glasses, trying to knock them off the shelves. When the Child Bride heard Jillian at the window—or perhaps she just sensed Jillian's presence, such are the powers of the dead—she turned and her hair rose away from her head as if a big Costco fan was blowing and just then Jillian could see through her and realized that the Deer's Head had done her a solid: old Wiley *was* one sick puppy but, too late, he was standing on the other side of the glass. He slid open the door: "Why hello, sweet thing. Wanna come in?"

"Don't eat any of those pills," the Dead Child Bride warned her, via some sort of strange telepathy, "or drink anything he gives you."

Jillian closed her eyes and remembered all the episodes she'd seen of *One Thousand and Three Horrible Ways to Die* in case there were any hints there for her to save herself. But which episode? Death by Impalement? A javelin through the eye? Where would she get a javelin? Death by Decapitation? Not likely. Death by Electrocution, a possibility, since every house had electricity, and then she remembered the one where the guy who was out on parole got an apple shoved in his mouth, he was tied up, trussed up like the pig that he'd proven himself to be. Death by Dominatrix, she thought it was, but she'd closed her eyes so she didn't know exactly how he died, only that it was an excruciating death which seemed, in her opinion, a fitting way for Wiley to die, too, being as it was like Biblical, an eye for an eye and a tooth for a tooth and all that.

And then, as if both the Deer's Head and the Dead Child Bride had seen her thoughts, when she opened her eyes, that was indeed the scene in the kitchen. The Deer's Head had gone inside and was floating up near the ceiling shooting lasers from its eyes which somehow pinned Wiley to the wall and the hands of the Dead Child Bride now moved so rapidly as to be only a blur and Wiley's open mouth had a waxy tangerine stuffed in it. His eyes were bulging out and, behold, unbeknownst to anyone, one of his eyes was glass and it popped out and rolled across the floor to the open door where Jillian was standing.

"Run!" the Deer's Head said to her.

"Run," the Dead Child Bride said, "*Run!*"

Jillian picked up the eye, which was still warm and slightly moist, and ran.

5

The Dead Child Bride has not always been dead. She remembers, when she was little, how she loved to sit on the lip of the tub before her bath and tip her head back and feel her hair fall down her naked back. She used to move her head from side to side so she could feel her hair like a waterfall or like a big feather; she moved her head so she could tickle her own back, so she could give herself goosebumps. She remembers other intensely pleasurable things: cherries bursting in her mouth, cold sweet ice cream, the smell of earth when she made mud pies with her brother, the buzzing bees in the lazy garden, running with her strong strong legs, riding bikes, riding in the car with the windows down, wind wind wind wind whipping her long dark hair all around. And thus it was when she died, a wind came and lifted her and she could see, as if she were flying over the whole world, all the other dead child brides—although not all of them were dead, and not all of them were children, and not all of them were brides: a little girl who had been taken through her bedroom window; a woman's head sticking out of the sand, men gathered around her, arms raised, stones in their hands; women in courtyards, their voices rising in grief; women in apartment buildings, five locks on every door; girls in cars, girls in bars, girls in shopping malls, girls in army uniforms. It made her dizzy.

And now Jillian. And now, again, Wiley. The Dead Child Bride, her heart is cold, she freezes him. She manifests her face as it is now, a skull, the smooth bones, the eye sockets, one caved in where he hit her. "The orbital bone," she says to him, her voice frosty. "Can you say that, Wiley? Or-bit-al?" She comes so close to him that he can feel the ice in her voice, he can feel that she is not afraid, and then her hair, her long black hair which, in death, has been growing longer and longer, her long black hair, strong as silk, it reaches out like tentacles and strangles him. It is that easy.

In the Precarious City

In which Jillian travels to the precarious city and encounters the ghost of her great-grandfather, among others.

1

Angie O'Malley and her daughter Jillian are on a plane, its shadow skimming the clouds below them all the way to San Francisco, a city Angie considers precarious, as in "an earthquake could happen at any moment." She's been worrying for weeks that the big one will hit while she and Jillian are there. The history of San Francisco, at least for her, is bound up with her mother who grew up across the bay and now lives near Telegraph Hill. San Francisco!—where her grandfather had a mistress for thirty-five years before leaving her grandmother who was the mother of his nine children.

This, according to Angie, is how the leave-taking happened. Her grandmother got a bill from the cleaners for the other woman's drapes and so, feeling ill, she climbed the long curving flight of stairs to her bedroom—the house was a Victorian, Angie tells Jillian, just as her grandparents themselves were Victorians of a sort, born in the days of Queen Victoria, formed by those morés, his infidelities, therefore, however sordid and hidden, a fact of life. Still, her grandmother felt disturbed and this disturbance was wrenching unto the very cells of her brain and so she lay down on her bed and had a stroke. Her husband found her there and sat by her side all night. He sat there, waiting patiently for her to die, calling no one, even though his son the doctor lived in a house nearby. When, by morning, his wife had turned blue but was still breathing, he went downstairs, knocked on his oldest daughter's door and said, "Your mother is ill. She needs you." And then, free of the burdens of his life, he disappeared with his mistress into the precarious city forever.

Angie has told Jillian about her great-grandfather before but because Jillian can't talk, Angie has told her lots of things in long convoluted monologues that Jillian allows to drift through her mind like clouds streaming across a summer sun, like geese flying south, like dark fish beneath the surface of a pond in winter.

Jillian looks out the window of the plane. They are above a layer of clouds dense as cotton batting. She can't see through them. Is this heaven?

Even so, Angie continues, my mother, your grandmother, the youngest of the nine and so, perhaps, the most innocent, adored him. *Adored* him! Even though he left her mother when she was eighteen. Even though he'd been the kind of college student who found it amusing to use his fountain pen as a dart which he chucked with surprising accuracy into the scalp of the bald guy who sat in front of him. Even though he'd bragged that the Chinese laundry-man always put exactly the right amount of starch in his shirts because he'd threatened to cut off his ponytail—or queue—if he didn't, which meant, Angie explains, depending on whose story you believe, the laundryman would either never get to heaven or could never return to China.

2

Ha! Jillian thinks, rolling her eyes at her mother, that shows you how much your grandfather knew! Han Chinese men hated to wear queues—they had been forced to shave the front of their heads and braid the remaining hair into a queue in the 1600's by the Man-chus in the Qing dynasty. To rebel was a sign of treason, punishable by death, death by beheading. And thousands—tens of thousands? hundreds of thousands? does anyone know for sure?—lost their heads, literally, rather than put their hair in a queue. Blood had run in the rivers, as they say, soaked the thirsty earth.

Jillian knows this because in those moments when she was first born, in those few precious moments of omniscience, the universe had downloaded into her brain all sorts of random data. Her hard drive is wired wired wired; it's her retrieval system that lacks some precision. For instance, when she thinks "queue," she thinks "Qing," and when she thinks "Qing," this catchy little saying starts playing: *"keep your hair and lose your head, or keep your head and cut your hair."* Which, in a way, makes no sense, she thinks, but then who said oppressors had to make sense? Even historically?

Of course, if you were Chinese in America and didn't have a queue, you couldn't go home to your family in China, but by 1911 and the Xinhai Revolution, all that had changed and so she can just imagine the laundryman looking up at her great-grandfather, all six feet four inches of him, and thinking WTF? *Dude.* It's the 1920's. Even the Emperor has cut his queue.

At that moment, her own faulty brain is flooded with images from *Bonanza.* The little Chinese cook—what was his name?—he had a queue. And a cleaver. Hop Sing. Oh, how she loves Little Joe.

3

The girl is different. Even I can see that. She must be nine or ten, almost as tall as her mother, and yet she sits there looking out the window at the bridge, drawing like a much younger child, while her mother and grandmother drink tea. Lois, her grandmother, my boss, insists on calling me María. This has been going on for years. ¿Por qué? Marisol is too hard to remember? The girl's mother smiles at me apologetically when I set the tea before her but then, just as quickly, she drops her smile and I am left wondering if I am seeing things. These people. A cloud across the sun, that quick they change, as fickle as the weather here in the area of the bay.

Later, she—the mother, Angie—she says to me, "Where did you learn to make scones like these? I didn't know scones were Mexican." This is a joke?

Lois, she talks about her other daughter, the one with the broken heart whose husband absconded with the teenager from his morning math class. She says, "And what is the common denominator? She is. She drives them all away."

"*Mom*," Angie says, and I know what she is thinking because I've heard it all—the first one liked to powder his nose, coca, the second one, too fond of drink, and this one, the third, according to Lois? Not marriage material. Or not the marrying type? How does she say?

Angie, she motions with her head towards the girl. Why? Because she thinks her daughter is too young to hear of such things as an uncle who likes girls her age? I can tell you this girl knows of such things about men—as all girls do. Why pretend otherwise?

"He's a p-e-d-o-p-h-i-l-e."

"You can't keep a man with vinegar."

"Oh, *Mom*. But why would she want to keep him?"

"I'm just saying. My brother was seventeen years younger than his wife. Who happened, also, to have been his teacher in high school. A lovely woman."

The girl looks at her mother and then at her grandmother and then at me. She isn't an imbecile, this girl. In fact, like me, she sees and hears everything. She's maybe too smart, this girl. On her paper she is drawing the ocean and the sun but I don't know if it's the view out the window or my name, mar y sol, sea and sun, that she's drawing. Maybe, since she can't talk, it's her way of saying my name in Spanish because she follows me into the kitchen and gives it to me but when

I put it on the refrigerator with a magnet, she takes it off and folds it up and puts it in my hand. And then she sneaks another scone.

When Lois says, "Thank you, María. What would I do without you, María?" I know it's my cue to go to the foyer and get my bag. I hear her whisper to Angie, "What *will* I do if we get a law like that one you have in Arizona where all the Mexicans have to go back to Mexico? I can't afford an Oriental, not one that speaks English."

And then she calls, "Take the leftovers home, María, to your little ones because we, here, we do not need to eat sweets and those scones are loaded with butter and we are watching our girlish figures, aren't we girls?"

I know she is looking at the girl, Jillian, who is at that age where the chubbiness has not yet become breasts or hips and at her daughter whom she thinks is not doing a good job because she let the girl eat four scones—not counting that extra one in the kitchen—and drink two cups of hot chocolate with lots of whipped cream but, of course, the chocolate is very good. It is from Mexico.

4

Jillian has stopped in front of a store called the Memory Gallery. She is gazing at white cartons like take-out containers for Chinese food, there are lots of them and they are suspended from the ceiling by invisible strings and so they seem to be floating in the air. Jillian studies her reflection in this storefront window, which is a gloss over the white containers hanging inside, the scrolls and the mannequin in the red Chinese dress, the photographs of old Chinatown which are propped up in the window and seem eerily familiar. In the reflection, she sees behind her Chinatown in the morning, the street nearly empty, and her grandmother pushing her walker. Hunched over, she looks just like a little Chinese lady, even her tightly-permed black hair, even her red sweater, and the walker makes the walking so slow that Jillian has time to look at herself in the windows, at the dragons on the light posts, at the bins full of vegetables she's never seen before, light green and looking like large sea cucumbers or fantastic turds of fantastic lizards, maybe of Komodo dragons or Gila monsters, and the dried brown things in bins that look like the husks of cicadas and might cure anything if they didn't stink so much. Will someone make her drink tea? It is a possibility.

She turns from the window and across the street, there is a building like a huge pink pagoda and a Chinese girl is leaning out of an upstairs window and she is brushing her teeth and Jillian looks at her, wonders if she's just been imported from China or if she is a ghost who is always hanging out that window, brushing her teeth. The world swirls, a kind of upside-down whoosh like when you look up too quickly and the buildings topple in and the clouds move fast and inside you are falling, like that, a *whoosh!* her insides swirled upside down, and when she recovers her balance, there, on the walk in front of her is her great-grandfather. Does anyone else see him? Her mother and grandmother have walked on, the grandmother, who *adores* him, lifting her walker, lifting her walker slowly in front of her, methodically in front of her. She seems to see nothing.

Her grandmother and her mother and herself—Jillian looks at her own hand—they are the only ones who are still in color. Everyone else is like a photograph from the Memory Gallery come alive: her great-grandfather is there and the other men, some kind of officials with their black coats and little square hats, and the Chinese women dressed in long dresses just like Kitty in *Gunsmoke*, well maybe not so much cleavage, and the men are asking for the women's papers because they are Chinese and whether they are citizens or not, they have to carry papers because, as her great-grandfather explains to her, you can't tell by looking at them. They all look alike, he says, those Chinese, those inscrutable Chinese, those clever Chinese, and so they have to carry papers because the Workingman's Party wants to exclude the yellow hordes, the Mongol hordes who take all the jobs and smoke opium and gamble and sleep with prostitutes, who bring their ways which are not our ways across the ocean and, really, they bring the mice and the lice and the plague and take over all the gold claims and do we want miscegenation? No! It should be illegal. If a white woman marries a Chinaman, he says, she should lose her citizenship. If a white man kills a Chinaman, over a gold claim, say, another Chinese cannot testify against him. We cannot have, in a court of law, a Chinaman testifying against a white man. If a Chinese doesn't have a resident pass, he should be arrested, sentenced to one year of hard labor, and then deported and made to pay for his deportation. Thus sayeth the Workingman's Party and the Golden State of California.

Thus sayeth her great-grandfather who was born the same year as the Exclusion Act and so believes it is as natural as breathing to want to cut off a man's pigtail, who is standing before her and seems to recognize her because he holds out his hand and says, Jillian! I've been watching you. Why you *are* your grandmother's granddaughter! You have the same twinkling brown eyes and the same fanciful imagination! Let us go and drink the tea that is made from dried ginseng that looks, a little, yes, like the dried husks of cicadas, but is not. Ginseng and ginger will do you good, my dear girl. Why did your mother marry that Mexican? And why did they take you away to that god-forsaken desert?

But Jillian sees her grandmother and her mother far up the sidewalk now, up near the crest of the hill, and she does not want to be left behind at the turn of another century where there is no such thing as the Good Old Days no matter what they show on *Bonanza* or *Rawhide* or *Gunsmoke*. It's all the same as now, just ask Marisol, she thinks, who has fled Mexico and the rolling of heads there, and so she runs up the hill to her grandmother's red sweater but when her grandmother turns around, it is not her grandmother, it is a little old Chinese lady with freckles dusting her face, and she seems to be glaring at Jillian. It's a glare, Jillian is sure, she is sure this little old lady does not like her.

And then she looks up to see if her great-grandfather has followed because she suddenly needs to know: did you really want my great-grandmother to die? Was that what you were waiting for? Why you let her turn blue? She remembers the dark eyes and deep dimples of her great-grandmother in the picture on her mother's dresser and she remembers the ponytail, that switch of her great-grandmother's thick black hair, her beautiful hair, that her mother keeps wrapped in silk in a special box in a special drawer. *Did* you?

But he is gone and instead, Jillian sees a church and on the church these words: *observe the time and fly from evil* and the little Chinese lady is still glaring but now, she is no longer Chinese, she is Jillian's own fierce grandmother with her sharp nose and precise lipstick. Lois. Glaring. Because Jillian has nearly knocked her over and one broken hip is all it would take.

5

It is a precarious city. At any moment, the earth could shrug and the tall tall buildings would topple, the glass falling in sheets and shards, shattering bones, shearing flesh, heads lopped off neatly. Or not so neatly. The ocean could rise, fire could rage as it did after the 1906 quake when all that saved little Italy was blankets soaked in red wine. This is what Jillian is thinking, although not in these exact words; no, she is thinking in images and impressions. Glimpses of disaster come to her and she is momentarily dizzy with the precariousness of it all and therefore, with the brazen courage it must take to live in such a place, and therefore, when she rides the cable car with her mother and hangs off the side, she laughs at the smiling Chinese students in their neat school uniforms as they hang from the other cable cars coming from the other direction. She holds out her hand for a high five. They are all laughing as they slap at one another's hands. Because: why not?

The Astonished Dead

In which Jillian encounters the astonished dead and comes to understand both the shooter and the dead, although not completely.

1

Angie O'Malley has taken Jillian out of school for the afternoon for two reasons. One, it is chocolate cake day, their treat. Two, she needed to meet her sister Glenda, who is having marital problems and Angie thinks of herself as Glenda's first responder. Three, Jillian's teacher has been complaining, again, about her drawings. Okay, that's three reasons. As if Angie needs reasons. Her mother once took them out of school so they could go see an old matinee at the movie theatre. What was it? Something totally inappropriate for first graders, if Angie remembers correctly. *Night of the Iguana? Who's Afraid of Virginia Woolf?* Her mother loved Richard Burton. Just the sound of his voice, her mother used to say, that sexy Welsh voice. No wonder Elizabeth married him so many times!

Angie and Jillian pick a big white table under a mesquite tree that is strung with little white Christmas lights. Very festive, Angie thinks, although the small, furry dog strolling from table to table strikes her as an unsanitary touch—but it's the owner's dog and the owner is French, so what can you do? C'est la vie!

"We could order," she says to Jillian. "You know your aunt will be late."

Jillian pulls out her artist's tablet with the offending artwork but, instead of sketching, she leans her head back, her face towards the sky, eyes closed.

"All great artists," her mother tells her, "are misunderstood in their lifetimes."

Jillian doesn't answer. That she has simply never uttered a word or a sound is a mystery, even in this day and age of medical miracles, a fact that Angie and Jillian have accepted. Just as Jillian accepts, although her mother hasn't a clue about this, that she sees the dead. Oh, not all the time, not like in that movie, and they don't scare her. Just at particular moments, she is aware of them. The newly dead, the dead-for-a-long time, the oh-so-sad-dead, the tricky dead, and even the astonished dead. They are the ones she is drawing.

Hieronymus Bosch, her mother thinks. Can't that dimwit of a teacher see it? The clusters of grapes larger than some of the human figures, the giant fish, the intertwined lovers, the bird swallowing a man. Okay, so a few look like tortured souls. But Jillian, she is sure, is a genius.

2

Angie looks a little surprised when she sees I'm with Glenda, but Glenda asked me along because, as we all know, Angie is such a butt-in-ski and Glenda wants me to run interference. Marriage, infidelity, divorce, that is the boring topic of our conversation as we sit in the garden restaurant eating cake, specifically Glenda's decision not to divorce her husband Steve.

"We've been together ten years," Glenda says, "and so I have to ask myself, what are a few misguided moments? It was just a short-lived midlife crisis."

"At least he didn't buy an expensive sports car," Angie says. "You'd be paying the interest on that forever."

"Women have forgiven worse," I say and I list them: "Hillary, Tammy Wynette—although *why*? I haven't the foggiest."

"I would draw the line at boffing fifteen-year-olds," Angie says, "especially when it endangers your career. He's not a postman or a trucker, Glennie, he's a teacher."

"But it's over! Finis!" And then, from defiant to petulant, "I *love* him." Sheesh! Bad as a lovesick teenager. What is it about losing a man's interest that makes some women cling all the harder?

"I loved Bobby, too," Angie says, "but there are things you can't live with. And *he* didn't run around with little girls."

Glenda has nothing to say to that and neither do I. Although, ouch. Angie can be a tad judgmental. So we don't talk. We just eat. Until the cake is mere crumbs and smears of chocolate, until the water is sweating in the glasses, and until Jillian, Angie's retarded daughter, has gone back to drawing in a big notebook—little decapitated Indians, from the looks of things.

"How did he get away with it?" Angie asks. "The parents *say* they won't press charges, but do you believe them? I mean, your assets are his assets. Is it going to come back and bite you in the ass? Does the school know? Aren't you an accessory after the fact?"

"I can't be compelled to testify against him, can I?"

"Not as long as you're *married* to him."

I look at Angie. She watches the implication fly right over her sister's head. Because who wants to go there? Not Glenda. And not everyone's like Angie who says what she means and does what she says. Word is she gave Bobby one chance to go to counseling or AA and he didn't and so she was done. That was Angie and she had stuck to it.

"Stevie Sr. has proven himself to be not only immoral but also stupid," she says to Glenda. "You really want to stay married to someone who's stupid?"

The girl looks up from her drawing. She's just impaled a small figure with a javelin.

Glenda shrugs.

A wuss with Steve, a wuss with her sister, a wuss forever and ever, Amen.

"Wine time," I say, trying to lighten the mood a little. The shadows are getting long; the cake, as I said, is long gone; and Glenda looks about as gloomy as I've ever seen her.

"Don't tell me. He's been crying," Angie says. "Never trust a man who cries."

"Of course, he's been crying," I say. "What else can he do?"

I motion to the waiter and ask for a carafe of something with a little alcohol and a little carbonation. He is so cute—some flavor of Latin, hair in a messy ponytail—he says he has just the thing.

"You know, the new feminine male. The sincere male." I roll my eyes. "The *spiritual* male."

"Self-serving as ever," Angie says. "Just watch Fox News."

"Excuse me, you two," Glenda chokes out, "but I think you could be a *little* supportive."

"I am being supportive," Angie says. "I'm telling you the truth instead of blowing smoke up your ass."

The girl, Jillian, gives Glenda a scrap of paper with a drawing. A woman entombed in a giant transparent eggshell. A man with a large grape for a head.

3

Jillian has just situated herself on the top of the monkey bar and is about to hurl herself forward in a spin when the commotion first breaks out on the playground. There are men yelling—they are construction workers—and some of them are yelling in Spanish and some in English and so the mixture of languages makes for a discordant music. From her perch she can see another man, this one is dressed in camouflage pants and a black hoodie, and now he is waving a gun around in the air and now he is climbing over the fence that surrounds the schoolyard and he is carrying a round plastic

jack-o-lantern and now he is shooting the gun. Pop! Pop! Pop! He is
shooting the gun over at a circle of second graders who have joined
hands and are playing an organized game, perhaps Ring Around the
Rosy or Farmer in the Dell. The children are singing and shouting,
as children do, still oblivious, and the man is yelling bad words that
you are not supposed to say about anyone or you will get in trouble
with the principal. He is yelling and shooting and the children don't
even break hands but start running this way and that, almost like a
school of fish or a herd of small confused horses. This way and that,
they are running and holding hands and screaming, oh! oh! oh! and
now the construction workers are climbing the schoolyard fence,
trying to get to the man who has put the jack-o-lantern down and
is shaking his gun and looking at it and then shaking it again as if
he can't believe the damn thing is no longer working.

Of course, the man can't see why his gun has jammed but Jillian
can. She can see the newly-dead woman who, still weeping and
weeping for her own lost life, has put her finger right in the barrel
of the gun. Both the weeping woman and the gunman are staring at
the barrel as if mystified. Jillian is not mystified, of course, because
in those few moments of omniscience when she was first born, she
saw, in fleeting fashion, like a newsreel on fast forward, all the vari-
ous ways people had killed one another through the ages. She saw
flying arrows blacken the sky and pots of boiling oil tipped from
the rampart walls, she saw berserkers run towards other berserkers,
swords thrusting, swords flashing, guillotine blades falling, Gatling
guns blazing, mushroom clouds rising. She saw the Crusades and
the Inquisition and the Holocaust and the Khmer Rouge, who sometimes photographed their victims right before killing them and then
piled their skulls in glass cases afterwards as if they were trophies.

Oh, the astonished dead! In those few moments of precious omniscience, she saw them, astounded by their own mortality: this is happening to me? *Me?* But I was the boy who liked to play with my sister's
dolls. Or the girl who loved oranges. How could this have happened

to me? No matter how it happened, the newly-dead always asked this, but they were especially astonished when it happened, not from disease or accidents or natural disaster, but at the hands of others, whether enraged lovers or fathers or soldiers or suicide bombers or mass-shooters or other types, like homophobes or misogynists or racists, who enjoyed torture, whose cruelty sprang from some well of dark inadequacy, doubt, loss of faith in their own worth or perhaps their own god—Jillian wasn't sure—or maybe from fear or guilt or blindness, a special blindness where they couldn't see the other human as human, like, say, slave owners who put bits in other men's mouths or vigilantes who poured salt in the water left for desert crossers.

Was there nothing one man would not do to another?

Maybe, she thinks, from up on her perch, as she surveys the scene with the Buddhist detachment she has tried to practice from birth, maybe this is why she cannot speak for if she were ever to tell other children what she knew, if other children were to have her knowledge, would they even want to grow past their own small baby-hoods?

But, yes, she thinks, watching the masses below her, they *would*: because not only did their parents cultivate ignorance, mistaking it for innocence, but like most people they believed they were the exception and would be spared. Just now, for instance, look at them running this way and that. They still didn't believe that anything like this could happen to them even though it was happening!

Jillian, on the other hand, knows anything is possible because the older siblings of these children come up behind her and jab her in the ribs just to see if she will scream in surprise or pain or they sneak up behind her as she sits at her desk and they quickly scribble over her drawings with their clumsy crayons to see if she will call out in protest—small examples of their possible future mean-ness, she knows, but poignant all the same.

As Jillian sits and watches from her perch, the teachers begin to gather their wits—for although the mayhem seems as if it has been going on for a long time, it has been only a few seconds or perhaps one minute—and so they also begin to gather the children and herd them towards the school building. Jillian can see now that some of the children are bleeding from their arms or legs, little trails of blood, although not from the head and, so, no, not to worry, no one is lying on the ground, no guts or brains have been spilled, no heads are rolling, and yet the wailing woman, seeing blood, begins to wail even more and, hearing her wails, more of the dead appear, rising from the ground, descending from the clouds, materializing even from the branches of trees. They surround the man with the gun but he just shakes it and then picks up the jack-o-lantern and begins walking towards Jillian although he does not seem to see her at all. Instead, he is looking behind her at the children streaming into the buildings.

Maybe he has some sort of bomb or other incendiary device inside that jack-o-lantern, she thinks and then, for some reason, she has no clue why because this has never happened before, she sees inside his head and inside his head she sees him in a place like a school and he is wearing a uniform and a bald man is swearing at him and taking keys away from him, and then she sees him in a grocery store and he is afraid, he pushes his cart without looking at anyone, and then she sees him in a room all by himself and he has lots of guns and he is watching the TV and the man on the TV is very upset, he is crying and pointing to charts and then looking at the man with the gun as if to speak right to him, pleading with him personally, and inside this gunman's heart a little version of himself is listening and it begins to shrink with fear, it gets smaller and smaller and harder and harder, like a raisin or a pebble, and it is rubbing there, causing pain, and so he starts loading his guns and shouting at the TV, saying all those bad words a person is not ever supposed to say unless they want to practically *live* in the principal's office, the N-word and the S-word and the F-word and the one Jillian especially dislikes: Retard.

Seriously? Retard? He is a dumb-ass dick-wad for sure—although she knows you're not even supposed to *think* those words, especially not if you're trying to practice Buddhist detachment.

The newly-risen dead, although they have not been able to stop the man, have slowed him down considerably. He is walking like a man through very hot molasses, he is walking as if his limbs are falling asleep, and so Jillian decides she has time for her turn on the monkey bars—she'd had to wait in a very long line, after all—and she throws herself forward and spins and spins and spins and, as she's spinning, although she cannot see, she hears the wailing woman begin to say *for as you do unto the least of my brethren* and she hears all of the astonished dead begin to wail because just what if, in their moment of need, the woman had been an already-dead and she had manifested herself and come forward to save them, to stop the bullet the machete the knife the rope the rape the words that burn the words that incite the words that kill?

And so the astonished dead are becoming the oh-so-sad-dead and the construction workers have tackled the man with the gun and they are yelling at him, in Spanish and in English, and they are pushing his face in the dirt and his teeth in the dirt. They are making him eat dirt, in other words, which is not so kind, Jillian thinks, but she understands the impulse.

4

The astonished dead are standing before her although, because she has spun so rapidly and so much, they are a little blurry. What would they say to her, if they could speak? They are chatting among themselves. They are glad to see one another, which makes her think that death must be a lonely place, even though there are so many of them. Can they touch one another? If not, it must be a *very* lonely place, for the body craves touch, she knows. She loves it, for instance, when her mother brushes her hair or even runs her fingers through her hair as Jillian lies, head in her mother's lap, while they watch TV. This, Jillian knows, is why people love to look at pictures of lovers and of mothers holding babies and it is why her Uncle Steve Sr. ran off with that girl even though it was a bad thing. The flesh wants what the flesh wants. It wants the touch of another person's hand in tenderness, it wants the warm sun, it wants the feel of wind in the hair. And swimming! The feeling of your almost-naked skin moving through cool water, the bubbles trailing from your outstretched fingers and tickling your face. She wonders if the dead miss swimming.

She studies their faces, wishing they could speak. Even though she knows that communion with the dead is never clear—which is why the living have such a hard time with the interpretation of the dead's words across the great divide of time. Just what did the dead mean, for instance, by liberty for all? Who was all? It wasn't *all*, even Jillian knows that much, at the ripe old age of twelve. And so do we really want to go back there to the Good Old Days of the Founding Fathers where a black man was 3/5 of a white man and women could not vote and the only good Indian was a dead Indian? She thinks not. She thinks the dead are optimists: they would never advise going back in time even though that means they would still be alive.

Instead, she realizes, the dead are not astonished *because* they're dead. No, they are simply astonished that the living take life for granted, that they do not value living—e.g. wind sun water good tomatoes and human kindness—over ideas. The dead are astounded at the man on the TV who plants the ideas and at the man with the gun who takes them into his body and is poisoned and twisted and they are astounded by the men who are forcing him to eat dirt and they are astounded by the people who will cheer the men who made him eat dirt, who will say, on the TV, "they gave him a little street justice," as if pain equals justice, as if justice justifies pain. She looks at the dead. They are fading and so Jillian decides to spin backwards. She wants to spin backwards, around and around, so she can feel alive in yet another way, and so she throws herself back and in that dizzy moment of the world tipping upside down, she can foresee a time when she just might have something to say.

¿Qué Horas Son, Mi Corazón?

In which Jillian and her mother travel to the Denver Gun and Knife Club and are nearly kidnapped by renegade cabbies.

1

Angie O'Malley and her daughter Jillian are driving across the Indian Reservation in Northern Arizona in the dead of night because Angie's sister has been in a motorcycle accident in Denver. Angie thinks it's ironic—there they are, risking their lives to get to Glenda and all because Glenda had risked her life to please her philandering husband. Sheesh! Everyone knows how dangerous it is to drive across the reservation at night. Even Indians will say so. Angie once had a friend who was Navajo and her friend had lost several relatives to drunk drivers and so Angie knows she isn't being politically incorrect, just honest.

"Never-the-less, here we are!" Angie says aloud. "In spite of my genetic predisposition to prejudice. Driving across the reservation at night!"

Jillian says nothing in response, naturally, but she does pat her mother on the leg as if to say, there, there, Mom. I know you're not racist. I know you're more complicated than that.

Angie's hands grip the wheel. Outside it is dark dark and, if they were to stop, the stars would wheel above them in a wide cloudless

sky, the land would stretch for miles and miles, the tall rock formations like ghostly ancient figures, beautiful, Angie knows, in the
rising or setting sun—oh, the colors, then—coral, rose, magenta,
purplish blue. At those times, when the light is just so, magical and
alive, she can imagine this land becoming a part of your heart, opening something inside you, but at night, it's just plain eerie. At night
the rock formations look like huge amorphous ghosts instead of
the igneous intrusions that they are. That's all they are, she reminds
herself, magma chimneys of old volcanoes, the sedimentary layers
of earth around them having been blown away during centuries and
centuries of the endless stinging wind.

"A long time ago," she tells Jillian, who is staring out the window, watching for cows or sheep or horses, that's her job, to be on
the lookout for large animals that might suddenly materialize from
the dark sides of the road and step onto the highway, "a long *long*
time ago, like maybe a hundred and fifty years ago, we promised
the Navajo an aqueduct. By we, I mean the federal government, of
course. But where is it? Tell me, do you see an aqueduct? No water.
What grows here? Nothing. Absolutely nothing. That's why they
have to herd sheep. That's why they're poor as dirt. No wonder they
drink."

And here, because she does not want to picture her younger sister
in a hospital bed hooked up to machines, she tells Jillian the story
of Mrs. Elliott whose car, when Angie was a girl, had hit a horse on
the road and the horse went through the windshield hooves first.
"And, so, since the horse didn't die immediately, it kicked and kicked
and Mrs. Elliott's face got the worst of it, according to your grandmother. All those broken bones in her face. She was nearly unrecog-
nizable, my mom said, she nearly died, her eyes knocked out of their
sockets"—Angie, with a lurch in her stomach, relays this particular
detail, although she does not want to even remember it—"and yet
her husband stayed by her side. He and the kids still loved her. They
loved her more, in fact, for having almost lost her."

Why does Angie tell Jillian this story? Poor Mrs. Elliott, so disfigured she would never look the same, her mother had lamented at the time—which was true, she never did, because this was back in the days before plastic surgery could work its many miracles.

"The point of this story," Angie tells Jillian, "is that Mr. Elliott still loved his wife. Unlike that schmuck, your uncle Steve, who was probably drunk or high on pot—who would put it past him?!—when he wrecked the motorcycle, flinging your poor Aunt Glenda off the back and into the path of oncoming traffic."

2

Of course the kid's name is Stevie Jr.—the night charge nurse and I agree—these people are nothing if not predictable. Stevie Sr. has filled the room with flowers and teddy bears and cheesy cards as if he's trying to convince himself he still loves his wife. But he won't even talk to her, won't touch her hand. Leaves the kid to do that while he stands and looks out the window or paces up and down the hall, snagging anyone who will talk to him.

"Darlin'," he says to me, "darlin'? Could you put a dab of this on her lips?" And he hands me a pot of lip gloss. Strawberry and sticky. Something a teenager might wear. "And clean her up a little? And do something with her hair? Her sister'll be here any minute and I know she'd want to look her best."

When the sister comes, she's got her daughter in tow, a shy girl in the pre-teen stages of life, a little chubby, especially next to her mother who, I can tell already, is a force of nature. She brushes the hair from her sister's forehead. She whispers to her, *Glennie, Glennie.* She kisses her forehead. There is still a little dried blood there, where she kisses her, from when they drilled for the bolts. Then she plants herself next to the bed as if she is staking territory and glares at the husband.

"First you have an affair and then you buy a motorcycle."

Affair, that's the first thing out of the sister's mouth. And I'm thinking: in front of the kids? but I'm also thinking: *hello?* Your sister never heard the phrase *donor mobile?* But then Angie, that's her name, says out loud what we've all been thinking: "You are a fucking idiot. You know Glenda had no business on the back of that bike."

The monitor goes off.

We all stare at it as if it can tell us what Glenda cannot.

"You're upsetting her," Steve says.

"Actually," I say, fixing the clip on her finger, "it's just this."

I tell the girl that it has to stay on her auntie's finger. "To measure her respiration," I explain.

But the girl removes it again. Like it's a science experiment.

Sure enough, off goes the monitor.

"See," I say when I put it back. "We need to leave it on."

I give her a look. She's old enough to know better.

"We were just going around the block," he says. "I told her to put the helmet on, but you know how she is about her hair."

Oh, right. Wait 'til this Angie reads the police report. He was speeding. He had an elevated blood alcohol level, not high enough to be illegal, but still.

"There was sand on the road," he says.

The boy, he gravitates to Angie and her daughter and all I have to say is, they are lining up against you, Stevie Senior. I may not be a doctor, but I am an accurate observer of human nature.

"Virginia," he goes to me, looking at my nametag. He is rubbing the back of his thick neck like he's thinking hard. "Virginia? Could you help with this?" He gestures at his wife's body beneath the covers.

"Don't change the subject," Angie says and then she lights into him. What comes out of her mouth next could clear a bar full of bikers.

The monitor goes off again. I put the clip back on. Angie pulls the girl onto her lap and starts weeping into her long messy hair.

"Uuhmmm, Sweetheart?" he goes to me. "I think she needs to be changed?"

And then he leaves the room. Taking Junior with him. And they go down to the cafeteria or out to Mac-a-dee's at the end of the drive or over to Outback on the next block. Each meal he'll inch their way further away from her, what do you want to bet, until one day they don't come back, and there she is: eyes beneath her lids like marbles rolling around; bolts in her forehead; trach; IV; of course, catheter; feeding tube; you name it. He doesn't even like to touch her hand. The boy does. The boy will play with her fingers, talk to her.

Angie picks up her sister's hand. "See," she says to her daughter, "we have to leave this on because it measures the oxygen in her blood. If the monitor goes off too many times, a nurse will have to come in to make sure she's okay."

The girl looks at me.

"I'm not a nurse," I tell her. "I'm a nurse's assistant."

"She's the one who does everything no one else wants to do," Angie tells her daughter. "She's the one who takes care of your aunt."

"That's true," I say, "I am an unsung hero."

But I'm thinking, Hooters. Now that the sister's here to take over, he'll take the kid to Hooters.

3

Jillian and her mother are eating in the dining room of the hotel where they've been staying. Caesar salad and a few gin and tonics for her mom, a big bloody steak for Jillian, just the way she likes it, although she is seriously considering becoming a vegetarian because of all that methane cows fart. She wonders, do pigs fart methane? Would she have to give up bacon? Do chickens? Certainly not fish. She is just dipping a fry into the ketchup when it occurs to her that her aunt may never wake up.

Suddenly her mother thrusts her plate to the middle of the table and, as if she has heard Jillian's thoughts, says, "She's going to get better. She has to."

Then she snatches one of Jillian's fries, eats it without ketchup, and knocks back the rest of her third drink.

"Ready to go?" she asks.

Jillian thinks not. She looks pointedly at her steak.

"I'll get you a treat at the hospital," her mother says. "Chocolate pudding."

Her mother is tipsy. Hence the cab.

There is a long driveway from the main street to the turn-around place where the cab drops them off. There is a McDonald's at one end and there is a sidewalk with wispy grass and cigarette butts littered in the grass and sad petunias in their flowerbeds. The sad petunias are closing their downcast faces because it is that eerie time between dusk and darkness and all the crazies from the psych ward and all the junkies from detox have come out in their hospital gowns to walk that long walk. Their gowns, billowing out over their hospital pants, seem slightly ethereal in this light; some of them are pulling their IVs on stands, some of them are buying cokes or standing in line outside wanting to buy cokes, and some of them are bumming cigarettes or smoking cigarettes.

"Welcome to Denver Gun and Knife Club," her mother says when the cab finally stops, for this is what the hospital is called, Jillian knows, and she knows, too, that the night before they got there some gang-bangers had burst into the ICU to try to finish another gang-banger off and that's why, now, someone has to buzz you in and buzz you out and why there are policemen in the lobby.

Every day they've been visiting and playing different kinds of music for Glenda. Mozart is supposed to be especially good as it organizes the brain waves, which Jillian loves imagining in this way: first, brain waves crashing on the shore as if in a tumultuous storm and then they turn on Mozart! and suddenly the waves calm down, they ripple in quietly, one after another, each with just a lip of white foam, the little sandpipers, their long legs, running gingerly along the edges. Back and forth those calm waves, back and forth, like kelp swaying in its bed, like tall trees in a forest, Glenda's brain waves are undulating in rhythm with nature and Mozart and, beneath that, her mother's voice is talking to Glenda, telling her how everyone loves her, how everyone calls, how she's going to get better soon, telling her, squeeze my hand, Glennie, squeeze my hand.

And her mother always thinks she feels something. She does! She says, "Come here, Jillian! Hold her hand? See?! She knows we're here."

But the doctors come in and talk about the Glasgow scale. There is no eye opening, there is no verbal response, there is only flexion to pain. Not good, this Glasgow scale. Not good, Jillian knows. Jillian knows there is something called posturing, which Glenda does occasionally, and which indicates damage to the brain stem. She sees the doctors shake their heads.

On this night, when Jillian and her mom walk into Glenda's room, they can see through the big window into the next room, like always, the curtain pulled around the other patient's bed, but tonight there is a light on the other side of the curtain and the doctors are moving. There are several of them, hovering around the bed, their heads bowed over the patient as if in prayer, their quiet voices behind their surgeons' masks, their scalpels and saws. They are preparing to harvest his organs, Jillian realizes, although she does not know how she knows this and she does not know how to take her eyes away from the shadows and she does not know how she knows that the patient is this ordinary guy, slightly balding, the smooth face of a person without worries, just out of the Navy, going to see his girlfriend. He was driving along a highway when a mile up ahead a semi crashes into another semi and through the air, out of a clear blue sky, the fender of one of the semis comes hurtling towards his car and lands with a crash on the top of his car, which crunches the top of his head, knocking him out, and sending the car careening through the guardrail and into an embankment. That was the last thing he saw, a huge hunk of metal falling from the heavens, and the last thing he thought: *what?*

There are ways to die, Jillian thinks, that no one has ever imagined. "What the hell?" her mother says, yanking the curtain around Glenda's bed. "Just because she seems like she's asleep, they think she can't tell what's going on? And look at all this crap!" She is gathering up Burger King bags that still smell of grease and onions and stale fries. Waxy cups with ice still melting inside. "What? Does he think the nurses want to clean up after him? Just because Glennie always did?"

Jillian knows this is her mother's modus operandi: irritation at everything, anger to chase away sadness. And who can blame her? But then the sadness settles on Jillian. She breathes in the dark clouds of sorrow that her mother exhales, she breathes it in like second-hand smoke and it settles there, just around her heart or behind her eyes, like the kind of headache you get from a shift in the barometric pressure. Oh how it weighs her eyelids down, making her want to close them.

A nurse pokes her head in. "Everything okay?" Then she comes in with her clipboard and starts clucking and checking things off.

She's one of those nurses, a real gloomy tune, who thinks it's her job to give the patient's family a dose of reality as if there isn't enough reality all around them, as if right next door warm and bloody organs aren't being packed into little ice chests, as if outside one junkie isn't telling another his latest sad story about how someone followed him from the methadone clinic and knocked him on the head and took his whole week's supply of medication plus his cell phone, plus his wallet, and left him there to die because he's diabetic and how it took them, at the hospital, a whole week to figure out that he needed insulin and so, on top of withdrawals, man, he'd gone into a diabetic coma, but at least, when he woke up, he'd been cured of his nicotine addiction, although he sure could use a smoke right now if anyone has a spare, although at seven dollars a pack, he laughs, he knows that isn't likely.

"And if she does wake up," Nurse Sin-Esperanza is saying, "she'll never be normal. She'll think a bike is a stove and a stove is a bike."

At this, Jillian's mother yanks the nurse by the arm as if she is a small and stupid child. Out into the hall they go. "She hears everything," her mother whispers furiously. "It's her one connection to the world."

But Jillian wonders what the nurse means. Will Aunt Glenda think a bike is *called* a stove or will she try to *ride* the stove? This makes no sense at all.

Although one would definitely be worse than the other.

4

Outside, while they are waiting for the taxi, Jillian's mother gives a disheveled woman a whole dollar for one cigarette and the woman, who has a black eye and her arm in a cast, sidles into a story about how her ex chased her down with his jeep. "As if I were a dog," she is saying, "no, worse than a dog, he wouldn't do that to a dog, he *likes* dogs, as if I were a..." But here the woman pauses because she can't seem to think of anyone or anything her ex would run down *except* for her.

Jillian's mother exhales a short exasperated sigh full of smoke, dismissing the woman and her story in one fell swoop, but Jillian is curious about this woman, why she would love a man who launched a jeep at her and then laughed as she ran behind a tree, as she tumbled into a ditch, as gravel lodged itself in the left side of her face. Love seems, therefore, mysterious indeed. Even the woman looks as if her story has knocked the breath out of her. But what could be any clearer than this epiphany: you are less than a dog to him, less than a jackrabbit in the road, less than even a lizard maybe.

And then the taxi. The taxi—Jillian is suddenly suspicious of all men, but who can blame her?—is the color of dried blood, rust edging the fenders. Windows down or no windows? It sounds like it's lost a muffler. And where is the sign? The little box that tallies the charge? And why are there two men in the car? The driver, an older guy with greasy blond hair and a scruffy beard, and the guy next to him, a young Mexican, shaved head, tats all up and down his arms and even on his neck. And when he turns to look at Jillian and closes his eyes, she sees eyes on his eyelids.

But her mother doesn't notice. She takes the last hit off her cigarette, knocks the ash off and, not one to litter, never ever, wraps the butt in a Kleenex, puts it in her purse, opens the back door and slides in. Jillian pauses. Her mother is in the car. She is searching in her bag for something. The two men are looking at her. Would it be impolite to decline?

"Jillian?" her mother says without looking at her. Her mother, oblivious, is turning on her cell phone and so Jillian slides in next to her.

When they get to the end of the drive, the man turns left. Left is the wrong way, Jillian knows, left is the opposite direction of the hotel. The hotel is to the right. They have always turned to the right. Outside they are driving through a neighborhood that Jillian has never seen before. She is looking for landmarks. She knows this is supposed to be a bad neighborhood. This is the neighborhood where the gang-bangers live, the very ones who came into the ICU with their guns drawn. Maybe the Mexican guy in the front seat is a gang-banger—she studies the spider web on his neck and wonders why he wasn't more original in his choice of designs and wonders if maybe he lives in this neighborhood, if maybe there is some reason they are taking them into this neighborhood, if maybe the web is a sign, some web has been spun, some horrible gang initiation where they have to abduct mothers and daughters from hospitals and then rape them or shoot them or cut their pinky toes off with dull wire cutters. She is sure, in the history of the world, such things have happened.

But she doesn't see bad guys outside of the car, waiting, doesn't see knots of gang-bangers chilling on the street corners. Instead she sees small houses and green lawns and green plastic lawn chairs and Mexican families with small round black barbeque grills, the fathers bending over them to turn the steaks, the mothers coming out with platters of corn on the cob still in the husks, the children running through sprinklers or riding their tricycles. Through the open window, she can smell the meat cooking and water on grass.

Finally, the cab, if that's what it is, comes to a stop and there is an old woman standing on the corner and Jillian hears her, she is humming a song and remembering bright birds. She comes from a place with bright birds and bright flowers, where people walk on streets made of round smooth rocks and they call out to one another in Spanish, Buenos Días, Buenas Noches, and the walls are painted a deep blue and a bright pink, and this woman folds her sweater around her even though it is summer, and Jillian thinks, if this man turns the wrong way again, I am going to grab my mother by the arm and we will jump out of the car and we will find this woman and ask her to help us.

But her mother is talking to the scruffy blond guy, telling him about Glenda, how she is the sweetest little sister and how she was so trusting of Steve that she got her heart broken and now her head broken, and Angie is so worried, distraught, really, she is distraught because how long it will take Glenda to wake up? Because the longer she's in the coma, the harder it will be, and no one, least of all, she, Angie, has any illusions that Steve will step up to the plate or stand by for the long haul. Oh, no. She is sure he won't and where will that leave Stevie Junior? And who will help Glenda? She may have to— and here Jillian's mother's voice breaks because whose wouldn't?— Glenda may have to learn to talk all over again and learn to walk and feed herself and who knows what else?

The blond man is nodding his head and Jillian can see his eyes in the rearview mirror. He is saying to her mother that he goes to the Church of the Green Door and he is making amends and "this boy"—he calls the Mexican guy a boy—"this boy, here," he says, "that's why he's along for the ride." The boy with the spider web on his neck looks at her and says nothing but his eyes are brown and soft like an animal's, guileless. The sadness in them is so deep that Jillian feels as if she will drown, drown in sorrow, in her mother's, in the Mexican boy's, and even in the blond man's because he is a man who has done things he is ashamed of, things he cannot undo or forget or forgive himself for doing. There is a heaviness around his heart, and he is trying to ease the heaviness by helping this boy, and Jillian can see now, he *is* a boy, maybe fifteen or fourteen, not so many years older than she is. He has been pulled into a room and tattooed by his uncles; they have put a gun in his hands. He is from a place in Mexico where he can never go back, where a man comes into a club late at night and the men who are with him have guns and they take everyone's cell phones and they put bottles of tequila on the tables and they lock the doors, and everyone stays because the man with money wants them to stay. He wants them to drink and so they drink, they dance, they even laugh and talk, but all the time they are afraid they will be noticed, singled out, or their girlfriend will be noticed—this is not a time when you want a pretty girlfriend or a lovely wife—but so they dance and laugh and drink until the lights go back on and their phones are returned and, later, if on the streets, if one of the girls who was there that night is pulled into a car, if she disappears, they will say nothing. Or maybe it is a man who will disappear. It is understood, if you are this boy, that you will do as you are told and you will not speak the names of certain people—los de la letra is how you must say the name you cannot say, you cannot say los zetas unless you want to be one of the disappeared—although they do not call them los desaparecidos. That was another kind of war, another decade, another country, fed by the hunger of another kind of greed. Here, where the boy is from, those who have disappeared are simply the nameless dead, the faceless dead, fantasmas que nunca estaban, their bones found later buried in lime, their heads found separately from their bodies, and so Jillian wonders about that, about being headless, the thin bony spine, how there are spaces between the white round bones of the vertebrae, how there are nerves inside, how the arteries pulse in the sides of the neck and feed precious blood to the brain. Oh, how delicate the skin of the neck, how smooth, how lovers caress one another there, how babies nuzzle their mothers there, how you might even put your hand there, on your throat when something startles you. Se lo llevaron, they say. He was taken, he was taken away, and not by angels. This, everyone understands.

5

¿Qué horas son, mi corazón? Glenda whispers this in her own dreaming sleep. Estoy perdida. Lost, I am lost. Je suis perdu. The words come from forgotten nooks and crannies, from songs and old stories, coming in ur-language, that language before language, but no matter, no one can hear her, her lips do not move, she is wandering out of time. Maybe, she thinks, although "thinks" is not the right word; still, a thought swirls like smoke, floats up, and she tries to hang on to it. Maybe Jillian can hear her, maybe Jillian's hearing is more acute for Jillian has always seemed to hear what others are thinking—this is what Glenda muses, eyes closed, Glenda, coming to the surface as if she were a lotus blossom, unfolding but not waking and then falling again as if into dreams, her eyelids so heavy, as heavy as rainclouds in winter, she cannot lift them and so she floats into memories. Jillian is a baby and not a baby at the same time, as can happen in dreams. She is the Jillian of before Stevie Junior's birth, the only one Glenda loved fiercely then, mi corazón, she called her, felt her a small pure version of herself, no not exactly, a pre-dream of herself or a dream of herself that had not been lost. Jilli was one of those small girls with shy eyes, one of those girls you wanted to gather up in your arms like tulips or calla lilies, fragrant and delicate and lovely, her cool tiny fingers patting your cheeks, stroking your forehead when you had a headache. When you had a headache, she could take it away. And so, when Glenda feels Jillian's cool fingers, is she dreaming about the past or floating towards the present? No matter, the when of things. All times are now one time, this moment. Glenda feels calm, as if her mind is flooded with light, as if the murky churning waters are clearing and she is rising again, towards the surface. Ya es la hora. Already. I must go. So soon. She sees three tulips like in that old fairy tale, three tulips that will tell the future, so beautiful, and all she has to do is choose one and look inside and, there, she will see her future. Yellow or red or purple? Purple. Purple is the one she chooses for it is the most singular, the most lovely and, there, inside the tulip, there is her future.

Oh.

Like the mother in the fairytale, she turns away.

She does not want to choose such a life for herself. She does not want this life.

End of Days

In which Jillian flees la migra with Marisol, encounters the ghost girls, and foresees the end of days.

1

"What can I tell you," Angie O'Malley is saying to her mother, Lois. "This is a sad day." She is arranging her sister's hospital bed so that it faces the window. This is in their mother's apartment in San Francisco, near Telegraph Hill, and so the window looks out over the tops of other apartments, some with their rooftop gardens, some with their TV antennas, out to the Bay, and if you stand on your tippy toes, just so, you can see the Golden Gate Bridge way over there on the far left.

Angie cranks the bed up so that Glenda is almost sitting. Glenda opens one eye and then shuts it when she sees her mother. No, this is not the life she wanted. Better to have been unplugged, she thinks but does not say for two reasons. Reason one: because sitting in chairs near her are her son and her niece. In fact, the faithful of her life are all gathered around her bed, her son, her niece, her sister, her mother, and the maid whose name is Marisol but whom her mother insists on calling María. They are all there, very pleased with themselves that they have brought her here to San Francisco on a small plane to recover from her motorcycle accident and her broken marriage and so how can she wish she were dead? Plus, the second reason she cannot say such a thing: she has not yet recovered the power of speech and so, like her niece Jillian, she is mute, and so even if she wanted to say such ungrateful words, she would not be able to. Is not physically able to. Which is a bitch, she thinks. The bitch of all bitches. To be incapacitated *and* silenced.

She opens both of her eyes and smiles at them. They deserve this smile, she knows, the faithful, those who love her, and she banishes from her mind any thoughts of her husband Steve Sr., Steve the unfaithful, Steve the philanderer, Steve the smooth speaking dog of false words and false sentiments, Steve the Dominionist who thinks his desires drive the universe. Or, conversely, that the universe should cater to his desires.

Let a cloud come over his head and rain down upon him greasy car parts, splatter his life with 10/40 motor oil, let his clocks stop and his dinners burn, let all the machinery of his life rise up against him, even his laptop, especially his laptop, that purveyor of pornography and false communion. She will save Stevie Jr. from such a fate, she vows. She must. He is only ten. There is still time.

2

In San Francisco it is raining. Always raining. This you learn quickly when you move here to the area of the bay. Where I am from, from Guanajuato, rain is a blessing and we would never complain about such a gift. But Lois, la viejita, is tired of her house being full of people because, yes, it is a small house, a small apartamento, and Lois is used to being alone with only her thoughts for company and with only me, whom she can ignore so easily, and sometimes, like today, with my nieta Bella. I sometimes have to bring Bella because her mother, the ex-wife of my son, is busy with the babies from her new boyfriends. This is the way it is in this country. The men are goats and the women, no cojones. ¡Ay! I will say no more.

Right now los niños are seated at the dining room table, drawing on huge pads of paper. Bella, I am sure, has never seen so many colors of crayons and markers. Not even in school do they have such riches. Ah, well. So it is a treat for her to come and it is a treat for Stevie Jr. to have someone to talk to because, even though Bella is only seven, she is very smart. La chica muda, Jillian, she does not seem to care one way or another, although sometimes she gives to Bella the evil eye.

Lois is looking out the window. "The zoo, maybe?" she is saying. "Maybe by the time you get there, the rain will have stopped. It's just a mist, really, not rain. Or you could go down to Fort Mason and walk along the bay and look at the sailboats—Stevie Jr. would like that, I'd think—and then you can walk across the bridge."

Her daughter Angie does not even look at her. This is how she ignores her. By fluffing the pillows behind her sister's head as if it is the most important thing to be done. "There's an earthquake in Japan, Glennie," she says, still ignoring her mother, "the largest in recorded history, and Mother wants me to take the kids down to the beach. Has she heard of the ring of fire?"

La viejita turns and looks at the children, perhaps hoping they will weigh in. "Would you like that? To walk across the bridge?"

"Tsunami warnings all along the west coast," Angie is saying to her sister who—¿quien sabe?—may not understand one word, "and she wants us on the bridge! You get an epicenter close enough to those supports and they'll snap like toothpicks."

Meanwhile, Bella is telling Stevie Jr. about Pípila, the hero of Guanajuato, who crawled with a piece of slate on his back and torched the wooden door of the huge warehouse, el Alhóndigas de Granaditos, where all the Spanish were hiding as if in a fortress and from where they were shooting down Hidalgo's men with impunity. Pípila, who was slightly deformed and who was, tu sabes, a man others made fun of, a miner, he thought of this idea of the huge piece of slate and the torch and that he himself would risk his own life to burn down the wooden door so that Hidalgo and his men could break into the fortress and fight the Spaniards and los soldados and free México. Bella is acting out all the parts for Stevie Jr. Now she is leaning forward as if she is burdened with the slate and now she is setting fire to the fortress and now she is stepping over the bodies of the fallen Spaniards and now she is a campesina dancing afterwards in celebration.

"Later," Bella is saying, "the Spaniards cut off Pípila's head and they hung it in a cage and they took it from town to town for everyone to see. Like this," and she begins to walk around the room, holding up a cage con una cabeza adentro.

La viejita Lois is not pleased with this story, I can tell. She cocks her head and looks at me. "María," she says, "surely Bella would like to go on a little outing, too."

"Oh, I can just see it," Angie says, "I'll be standing on the Golden Gate Bridge with three children and the San Andreas will go and that bridge will fling us into the freezing water. The *shark*-infested freezing water."

"She has quite the imagination," Lois is saying to me of Bella. She means it not like a compliment.

"That is our history," I tell Lois. "There is a statue to Pípila in the hills and from the statue, you can see all of Guanajuato. This statue, it is a little like your Statue of Liberty, no? Maybe like that. It reminds us of the promise of freedom."

But I do not tell her what it says on the pedestal, Aun Hay Otras Alhóndigas Par Incendiar, which means "there are always other granaries to burn." Lois does not like to think there are histories other than the one she believes, pues. Just like people here in the area of the bay do not like to think of earthquakes. Yet there is no stopping the buckling of the earth when tectonic plates move. There is no stopping the surging of the sea. The earth is not finished forming itself. They know this, that the earth can shrug and the oceans will rise and the buildings will fall and, no matter how recently they have been retrofitted, the glass will rain down, and the people will scurry like ants. There are things men cannot prevent. They know this although they do not want to admit it. Just like they know the stock market could crash because of illegal bundling or los pobres could rise in rebellion or they, themselves, no matter how rich, could choke on a falafel and there they would be, helpless, choking, a glass of water an arm's length away.

3

Marisol takes the children out of the apartment and down to the bakery but when they return, clutching their bags of pastries, right there, outside the apartments, there is a van humming like a hive of furious bees and two men in green buzzing around.

"La migra," Marisol breathes to Bella, and then she herds them right around into a store where she buys them "I ♥ San Francisco" hats, sunglasses, and disposable cameras. "Today," she says entirely too cheerfully, giving them each a hat, a pair of dark glasses, and a camera and donning a hat and glasses herself, "today we are playing a game of tourists. Take pictures of that which captures your eyes!"

Then they hurry away from the store towards Washington Square where there are crowds of people, many of them brown, and so they mingle, hoping for invisibility, waiting for la migra to go away. There is a whole group of Chinese people, mostly old, and they are doing Tai Chi, moving their arms to the right and to the left in unison. Now they are clapping their hands. Now they are looking at the sky.

What catches Jillian's eye: there are so many people taking pictures of other people! This woman, for instance, Jillian takes a picture of her taking a picture of another woman in front of the Tai Chi people. Both women are dark-skinned, but the one taking the picture is sad—Jillian has no idea how she knows this, but it is the woman's voice she hears—*for us, it was like living in the dark*—and the voice brings with it a series of images, the woman when she is young, maybe sixteen, she is wearing a white dress like a sari, it is wrapped around her and she is very very thin. Her mother is telling her to go with the man: Go with him, it is better that you go away from me than that you starve here. Go, so you can have children and feed them and they will grow strong. The man takes her over the ocean in an airplane to a small apartment and at first it is a new life, but more and more he leaves her alone and his voice becomes harsh and so why had she come with him? Didn't she know she would miss her mother? Did her mother know he had another wife? *Here it felt like the end of the world, here there were no elders. Here men can humiliate us. They think they are the only humans with full rights.* How could his heart have become so twisted, Jillian wonders. But maybe it had always been that way. After all, would a good man take you away from your mother? Or wouldn't he bring your mother, too?

The old Chinese are clapping their hands again. They are moving all in unison, reaching up to the sky, then slowly circling down to the earth and, for a moment, it looks like a dance and Jillian is reminded of the dragon float in the Chinese New Year's parade, a giant dragon with lots of little human feet underneath, and she doesn't know why but she expects to see a huge flock of pelicans or seagulls or some other birds with large white wings swoop down and pick it up and carry it away and she remembers how the seagulls flew inland and saved the Mormons from locusts so they wouldn't starve and she remembers her mother's stories of the Irish potato famine, which was so long ago she doesn't even know how many greats to put before the grandparents that came over, great great great, maybe, or great great great great. They were on ships and they were lying in the hold below where it was dark and smelly and they were so sick and once they got here there were signs that said NINA, *No Irish Need Apply.* So this is how it always is? She wonders. Like *Angela's Ashes,* that book her mother had read to her: out of the frying pan and into the fire? You leave your mother, you escape starvation only to live in a dark apartment with a man who has a hollow heart?

But the two women, they are gone, and Marisol has walked ahead with Stevie Jr. and Bella, and Jillian hears the buzzing of the migra van and watches as Marisol shoos Stevie Jr. and Bella ahead of her, looks around for Jillian, perhaps, and then ducks into a Chinese grocery, one with huge bundles of green beans and bok choy and pale cucumbers in bins out front. Jillian wants to call out to Marisol. What about me? Wait for me! I don't have a green card or any kind of card and I can't talk!

But just then, as if someone has set the buildings on fire, out of the backs of buildings all around her, people are fleeing. So many. They come pouring out. There are so many of them that she can no longer see across the street to the Chinese stores. There are so many of them that no matter how quickly the men from the migra buzz around, they can't catch them all.

Jillian wants to run back to her grandmother's apartment and hug her mother. She can't imagine her mother leaving her alone on the street like this. She can't imagine her mother sending her away, not even if she were starving; not even if someone was pulling her mother's fingernails out with pliers, would she send Jillian away. No, Jillian is sure. If she was starving, her mother would pick plants from the desert and feed her; if she was drowning in an ocean, her mother would jump in and become a life raft; if she was falling out of a plane, her mother would become a parachute; if a man was shooting a gun at her, her mother would step in front of the bullets and, like Wonder Woman, zing them back at him with her furious kung fu wrists; if a speeding car was hurtling down the street and Jillian was standing in the middle of street and did not see or hear it, her mother would hold out her arms and shoot rockets of anti-gravity energy out of her fingertips and make the car fly up into the air and over Jillian; if a burglar came into the house in the dead of night, her mother would wake up instantly and konk him on the head with a cast iron skillet; if a man was looking at Jillian in a bad way and following her on the street, her mother would shoot lasers out of her eyes and blind him;

if a ghost was going to suck Jillian's breath away, her mother would stop it with one quick prayer. *Oh, no you don't,* her mother would say. But it is Stevie Jr. who comes instead. With all the fleeing and buzzing all around them, no one notices when Stevie Jr. takes Jillian by the hand and leads her to a taxi that is waiting in an alley. Marisol and Bella jump in the backseat next to them and, like in an old afternoon movie about WWII and the French underground, the four of them are whisked away.

4

In two years, when Angie is no longer afraid of the tsunami from Japan and Jillian is fifteen and her father has just died, Angie and Jillian will take their own photographic tour of San Francisco and Jillian will again take pictures of people taking pictures of other people. This time it will be just the two of them and sometimes Jillian will take pictures of herself taking a picture of her mother and herself. This will be less complicated than it sounds. She and her mother will be standing in front of a boutique, say, looking at the dresses and the bald mannequins and, there in the window, there will be their reflections superimposed over the skinny bald women in their neon dresses and if Jillian lifts her camera and takes a picture then she is taking a picture of herself taking a picture of her mother and herself. She loves the circularity of this equation. When they are sitting outside on the patio of the museum's café, she takes a picture of their reflection in the café window—they are, of course, sharing a slice of chocolate cake—and inside the café, the other diners look like ghosts eating in an afterlife of plenty. When they are in the sculpture garden on the roof of the museum, they stand in front of the spider by Louise Bourgeois, and Jillian takes a picture of their reflection, the spider's spindly black legs rising behind them in a slightly menacing way. It is not lost on Jillian that the spider, for Louise, represents the mother.

But on this day, Jillian is with Marisol and Stevie Jr. and Bella and they are on a grassy hill with a good view of the Golden Gate Bridge in the distance and Jillian takes a picture of an Asian brother taking a picture of his younger sister. His sister is jumping up in a cheer-leading position and behind her, the Golden Gate Bridge. And then the sister takes a picture of her brother: he is standing on a boulder with his arms just so, so it looks as if his top hand is pinching the top of the suspension tower and on his bottom outstretched palm rests the base of the bridge. Giant Boy Takes Golden Gate Bridge to Tokyo is the caption Jillian imagines.

Then Marisol leads them down a long path, up and down wooden stairs, along powdery dirt paths, the ocean to the right. Even though it is summer, here on the bluff above the sea, it is very cold and Jillian pulls her jacket more tightly around her and scrunches her "I ♥ San Francisco" cap down on her head so the wind won't blow it away. They are walking to Baker's Beach where they should be able to catch a bus and then go back to Telegraph Hill because by then, surely, the migra's vans will be full. These are the Batteries, Marisol tells them and then she tells how, during World War II, when Jillian's grandmother, Lois, was a girl living in San Francisco, they were afraid, not of Japanese tsunamis but of Japanese war planes and so here, under tons of earth, there were fortified bunkers with anti-aircraft guns. They'd been built way before WWII, way way before, Marisol says, but must have been re-fortified and manned during the war to watch for enemy planes and shoot them down.

"You know," she says, waving her hand towards the bay and then all the way around her, from one horizon to the next in a huge all-encompassing circle, "this was all ours, all owned by México until 1842, pues, which is why it's called el Presidio. San Francisco. California. Sacramento. Los Angeles. Nevada. Sierra Nevada. El Pacifico! Not to mention Santa Barbara, San Diego, y Avenida de las Pulgas!" Marisol pronounces everything in perfect Spanish. "¿Entiendes?"

It must have been lonely in the Batteries then, Jillian thinks, watching for those planes to appear, just as it is lonely now. There are very few people taking pictures of people here, in fact there are very few people period, and so Jillian is a little nervous. She wonders if any of the soldiers died out here, if their ghosts might linger. Plus, she has been reading Edgar Cayce and expects at any moment to see, walking down through the woods like an ordinary being, an angel or a demon. Why the angels and/or demons would appear only when humans were sparse, she doesn't know, but she suspects that angels and/or demons have had enough of humanity and so avoid crowds. There could be, for instance, around any corner, a man who slithers like a snake, perhaps he vomits nails or shards of broken glass, a sure sign of being possessed. Or there could be a woman who thinks she's the chosen one, the northern star, and is running for vice president, but who throws canned goods at her husband when she's angry and who encourages her harlot daughter to dance on TV. Harlot, Jillian knows, is an old word and not a kind one and she doesn't mean it, not really, but she's been reading about Satan and so it's the word that comes to mind.

Either way, as the slitherer or the star, demons are probably present, Jillian knows, you just have to look for the signs. Claiming that the Lord is on your side is a sign, she thinks, in fact a classic sign of arrogance and over-reaching, as is thinking you can use prayers to command legions of demons and send them to smite your enemies. Ha! Jillian thinks, what true Christian would want to command demons anyways? Or smite people, even their enemies? Isn't a true Christian supposed to turn the other cheek? Since Jillian is almost a teenager, hypocrisy strikes her as the deadliest of all deadly sins.

Just then a girl comes around the corner and appears in front of Marisol and surprises all of them. This girl is wearing a short black negligee and high heels.

"Do not look at her," Marisol says to Stevie Jr., "or you will go blind."

But Jillian looks. The girl is thin and her hair is long and dark and she is tripping down the path. Will her head spin around, Jillian wonders? Will green vomit spew from her mouth? But no, she seems to be a human girl and, behind her, a man with a big camera. Jillian stops in her tracks. Perhaps he is the demon for they can take many shapes, even portly and balding like this old guy who looks like he might greet people at the Walmart. The girl continues to trip in her high high heels towards the Battery where she stops and the man signals and she climbs up on the dark gray concrete, which must be very cold and hard. The man looks at her through the viewfinder and she arranges her face in pouty seductiveness and tilts her head and Jillian takes a picture of the man taking a picture of the girl in not-much clothing.

Marisol is pulling Stevie Jr. away from the girl very quickly for she doesn't want him to turn into a goat like her son's ex-wife's boyfriend, but just then there appears another girl! This one in thong panties and a lacey bra, that's all, beneath a see-through plastic raincoat, and another man, this one bald, yes, but young, with black plugs in his earlobes, has an even bigger camera. This girl finds a doorway to a bunker, flings her coat over a nearby boulder, and lies down, her back on the cold threshold, her long legs resting against the wall. She looks at the man and smiles and then she starts crossing and opening her legs as if they are scissors and then, just as Jillian raises her camera to take a picture of the second man raising his camera, a small ghost rises up out of the girl's chest and starts walking towards Jillian.

"Watch out," Bella says, "if you let her touch you, you'll never get rid of her. She'll follow you everywhere, even into the bathroom when you have to pee."

The ghost girl is such a waif. She holds her hand out to Jillian.

"I just want to be on the other side of the camera," she says, "like you are."

She has, Jillian thinks, a delightful accent. Russia? The Philippines?

But Bella moves in between them. *"¡Véte, ya!"* she says, stamping her foot and making a cross with her right hand. "Don't even think about it."

And so the ghost girl turns away but, instead of taking up residence inside the scantily-clad girl's chest again, she sits in front of her, elbows on knees, chin in her hands. "It's not at all what I expected," she tells them mournfully.

Bella rolls her eyes. "It never is," she says, leading Jillian away.

5

Back at the apartment, Lois and Angie have given Glenda a bath, they have washed and dried and brushed her hair, they have dressed her in a nice soft cotton gown, they have made salmon cakes and a chilled potato soup with fresh dill and are waiting for Marisol and the children to return with bread and pastries for dessert.

"I don't know how many times," Lois says, "I've told María that I want her to get a cell phone. If she had one right now, no problemo."

Angie has been sending messages through the air to Jillian: where are you where are you where are you? Think to me a picture of where you are, and I will come and get you. But to no avail. Where could they be? It doesn't take this long to go to the bakery, not even walking, not even with several detours, not even with three children.

"And now that I have to take care of Glenda," Lois is saying, "a cell phone is essential. What will I do when you're not here and I can't reach her? What if Glenda falls? What if I fall?" She shakes her head as if she is disgusted. "I'll just have to pay for it myself."

"Mother," Angie says, "you're getting ahead of yourself. Glenda can't even walk yet. Let's worry about one thing at a time." But, of course, she knows how worry is. One worry brings on another until, after a while, they all snowball and you can't separate the probable from the possible from the improbable from the impossible. A terrorist with a dirty bomb is the same size as a tsunami is the same size as someone kidnapping your child. You are helpless in the face of any of them. And who says they couldn't all happen on the same day? But what else is there to do? Glenda needs to eat and so they feed her the soup and salmon cakes and a few greens for good measure and Lois, while eating, seems to forget to be worried about anything more than her need for a nap, her need to have the dishes cleared and the kitchen cleaned, her need to have María as a permanent fixture in her life. She seems to forget that two of the missing party are her grandchildren.

While Lois and Glenda nap, Angie will go outside at least twenty times. She needs to walk off her anxiety which feels like battery acid sizzling through her veins. Where is Jillian? She walks up and down the streets looking for them, all around the block, over to the bakery, down to Washington Square, all through Chinatown, over to Coit Tower, over to Trader Joe's and, after each location, she zig-zags back to the apartment, but they are never home. It seems impossible to her that they could have been lost for this long. Hours! Jillian could have found her way home by now. She could have found a stranger and written down Angie's cell number, something. She could have written: Help! Unless. But who in their right mind would kidnap a little Mexican woman with *three* children?

What did Marisol do? Take them home with her and fall asleep? But who could blame her—she'd been working 24/7, sleeping on the couch ever since they'd arrived with Glenda. But why doesn't someone answer the damn phone? Certainly that chatty child Bella knows how to answer a telephone!

Stop, Angie tells herself, breathe. She sits on the steps outside the apartment, her legs and her mind exhausted. So what is a realistic fear? What could account for a three-hour trip to the bakery? If one of the children were hurt and they were at a hospital, Marisol would have called. If they'd witnessed a murder, she would have called. If—and here the battery acid that's been coursing through Angie's veins hits her heart—the Border Patrol. That's the only thing. Even *with* papers,

Marisol and Bella could be sequestered for hours or days, no phone calls, no word to the family. And *without* papers, they could be sent to Mexico, deposited in a border town or in the desert with no money, no way of getting home. And Stevie and Jilli? Do they even know their grandmother's last name? Or address? She's heard of things like this happening. Colorado, Nebraska, the meat-packing plants. California, when they disbanded the Bracero Program. History repeats itself all the time. They could be disappeared American-style.

She feels hollowed out with fear. She is like one of those crickets that, when a fly lays eggs on it, the eggs turn to maggots, the maggots burrow their way in, and eat the cricket's brain and heart and flesh. Only the exoskeleton is left, a husk full of maggot fear. A zombie cricket. This is who she is without Jillian.

6

On the bus, Jillian looks out the window at the Victorian houses, shoulder to shoulder, their steep steps up, at the wires for the cable cars and buses crisscrossing the sky, at the bland faces of apartment buildings, at the people on the streets pulling their shopping carts or their children by the hands. It is a long way to Telegraph Hill, she knows, and the bus is full of all sorts of people who get on and get off whenever they want. They are not like Marisol and Bella who are afraid. Bella, even though she was born here, is still afraid, still incognito, sitting next to the window, her hat pulled low, then Stevie Jr. in the middle, then Jillian, like three friends coming home from a school outing. Marisol sits up ahead by herself, so that if they take her, they won't take Bella. That's what Marisol had whispered before they got on the bus: if the migra gets on the bus and they take me, look away, Bella. Pretend you don't know me. Go home with Jillian and Stevie Jr. Call your father.

Stevie Jr. takes Jillian's hand and she sees that he has also taken Bella's and so there is a link from one to another which creates a transmission going straight to Jillian. Bella does not think she can look away if the migra comes. After all, it is her nana who folds her in her arms and plays with her hair now that her mother is so busy with the other babies and the boyfriend, the boyfriend her nana tells her to ignore. Don't go near him, Bella, she says. Do not let him touch you. Don't go into a room alone with him. And Bella knows it is true because of the way he talks to her mother, as if she is stupid, beneath him, when her mother is the one who works and puts food on the table and cleans the house and takes care of the babies. True, her mother cries a lot, which is annoying. True, she likes to go out with her friends and drink, but he comes with his friends and drinks and smokes and puts his boots on the table. He punches holes in the walls to punctuate his anger. Sometimes there are other men, not his friends, with guns, and so they have to move to a different apartment. Those times, her mother takes Bella and leaves her with her nana. Sometimes she leaves the little sisters, too, but she herself always always stays with the boyfriend. The stupid boyfriend. He has some kind of string to her heart she can't break, not even for her daughters. And what will happen if the boyfriend or the other bad men hurt her? And what will happen if the migra comes and they put her nana in the van with all those others, those others who have blisters on their feet from all the walking, and her nana is left in a town all the way down in México, even further than Guanajuato? And she will have no money and no one to help her.

Bella can't let this happen, she can't look away. They could make her nana wait for ten years to come back—Bella knows this has happened to others—it is a banishment, and when her nana tells about the others, she says, at least they have family but mine, mine is all gone. My family is gone from there or dead. No hay nadie. Her nana came here so long ago, when she was a teenager, her husband brought her, but now he is dead, too. My life is here, her nana always says. I had my son here and my nieta was born here, and aunque es un vida muy loca, es mía, and she smiles at Bella and Bella knows it is true. She and her nana are bound to one another by more than blood.

And Stevie Jr.? He does not want to go back to his father's house because the air is thick with remorse and guilt and anger. He does not want to live with his Aunt Angie and Jillian, although that's okay for the summer. He does not want to live with his grandmother, Lois, who scares him a little with her sharp words. He wants only for his mother to open her eyes and keep them open, to speak, to rise from the bed, to be his mother again. It's such a simple wish, he does not know why God can't grant it.

7

Jillian, who was given a few moments of omniscience when she was born, knows that when they get to Washington Square, everything will be as normal. The migra will have filled their vans and buzzed on to some sort of processing center, which will be filled with souls wailing, a sorrowful limbo she hopes never to visit. Instead, there will be people milling about the park, sitting on blankets while their children toddle around them, tourists taking pictures of street musicians, friends sitting in sidewalk cafés eating gingerbread cake and vanilla bean ice cream and drinking coffees with whipped cream. People with dreads will ask Marisol to sign a petition for seals or polar bears and she will wave them away as if they are flies.

When they get to the apartment, Lois will be on the phone because, upon waking from her nap and being informed of Angie's worries, she will have called the INS. "We can't sit by and do nothing," she'll tell Angie. "Who will change Glenda's diapers if we can't find María?"

And just as they walk in, the man on the phone is telling Lois, yes, he is sure they did pick up a María, at least one María today, but no, never in the history of the INS, he is sure, have they ever picked up a María with three children, two of whom are American and one of whom is mute.

"Never mind, here they are," Lois says, clattering the phone back in its cradle, for it is an old phone, heavy enough to be used as a weapon.

Jillian, whose omniscience is limited, suddenly sees her grand-mother's words in strings of electric green information, digitally, she guesses, like in *The Matrix,* crackling through the atmosphere, leaving bread crumbs for the buzzing men to follow. Can they want Marisol so much that they will come and break down the door? Can one little nana be so important? Has her grandmother, in her moment of need, put something in motion she cannot call back? But no one else seems to notice. Marisol needs to change Glenda and so the rest of them, to give her privacy, go into the kitchen to gather food for a smorgasbord, which is what her grandmother calls leftovers. It will be a celebration! They serve the cold soup and heat the salmon cakes, wash greens and tomatoes and carrots for a salad, gather chips and olives and crackers and cheese and chutney and blueberry pie. Her mother pours herself a large glass of chilled white wine, a small one for Lois.

"María?" her grandmother calls out, "Vino?"

And so they gather around Glenda's bed and eat, and Bella and Stevie Jr. tell of their adventures that day, leaving out the scantily dressed girls at the Batteries and the ghost girl. And outside, Jillian looks outside and sees earthquakes and tsunamis and hurricanes, the chaos of volcanoes and war and deportation, children crying for lost parents and vice versa. Buildings on fire, buildings falling into their basements, buildings floating on waves. There are motor-cycle accidents and cars crashing and people shooting guns. A sad person jumps off a bridge. A suicide bomber detonates himself in a crowded market and a child turns and opens her mouth to scream and bone fragments fly in and lodge in her lungs. Women in abayas search among the dead and wounded. Women are always searching among the dead and the wounded.

But here, here high on a hill in a small but expensive apartment, Jillian and her mother are together. They are safe, safe with everyone they love. Gathered around Glenda, they are eating food and drinking. Stevie Jr. and Bella are telling stories and the rest of them are laughing.

Dear Juana of God

In which Jillian makes a pilgrimage to Magdalena, Sonora, México, encounters Juana of God, and thus brings Marisol home to Bella.

1

It is not surprising, given the state of her world, that Angie O'Malley would look to Oprah for guidance. Of course, she doesn't actually turn to Oprah, not personally, but all the same she gives Oprah a shout out for inspiration, Oprah via her daughter Jillian. This is how it happened: Jillian was sitting on her Aunt Glenda's hospital bed in the living room—Glenda was asleep, earphones in, Mozart playing quietly on her iPod so the sonatas could rearrange her brain cells—and on the TV, this Mexican woman was shoving nasal probes up a man's nostrils to rid him of a brain tumor. Jillian let out a noise, a grunt maybe, but the closest she'd ever come in her fourteen years of life to a word. And Angie—hoping for a miracle—rushed in from the kitchen and saw Jillian, dear mute Jillian, pointing at Juana of God.

Angie took it for a sign. Not that she wanted anyone to shove anything up Glenda's nose, but there were other ways of performing miracles, she was sure, and there was a very handsome medical doctor—an American, Ivy League—on the show who showed a scar on his chest just below his ribs where he had spontaneously started bleeding after witnessing the near lobotomy. The doctor went on to tell Oprah that the experience had turned his life upside down. Upside down! Because, for one, the near lobotomy had made the guy's tumor shrink and then disappear. And for another, he, the doctor, now had to question everything, *everything*. His entire worldview.

The doctor shrugged. "Sure, maybe there's a logical, a medical, explanation. Maybe it stimulated the pituitary gland, maybe not. Maybe we will never know. But the tumor is gone. That I do know."

Here, a short film of the doctor and the man whose nostrils had been probed walking away from the healing. The man looked dizzy, woozy, as if he couldn't believe he'd just allowed someone to shove steel rods like knitting needles up his nose. The doctor lifted his shirt and streaming from a hole in his side, blood. He touched it. He touched it again, amazed.

"There are things we don't understand," the doctor went on, seated next to Oprah in front of her studio audience. "All things are mysteriously connected, this is what I learned. Empiricism is not the be-all and end-all."

Here, a panning of the audience to whom Oprah nodded and smiled, Oprah as solemn as she always is on occasions involving transformation.

Angie sat down and watched the rest of the show. What else could they do, but seek a miracle? The doctors here in San Francisco were offering nothing, nada, no hope for Glenda. Marisol, the woman who had been taking care of Glenda, had been deported. Angie had been helping her mother, Lois, take care of Glenda, and they were both utterly exhausted. Utterly. So in spite of the 10,000 deaths in Mexico in the last year alone due to the warring drug cartels, in spite of the stories about American women and Mexican babies being abducted and killed by drug dealers, their corpses being hollowed out and used as containers to transport drugs, in spite of all of that, Angie decided they would risk it.

After all, lots of people live in Mexico and don't get beheaded or stuffed with drugs or shot execution-style and dumped in pits of lime, and it's only a fifty-mile drive from Tucson to Magdalena along a four-lane highway, and the Angels in Green rove that stretch of road and stop to help stranded motorists. They don't do that here in the states, she thought. ¡No angeles verdes aqui! She popped a Xanax.

Dear Juana of God, she wrote at the top of the letter she would send ahead of them, and then she described Glenda's maladies of the mind and body and heart.

2

Magdalena de Kino, Sonora, México: brown hills squatting in the distance, then ranches and fields of green, and at the center lies the town and the lovely Plaza Monumental with the Temple of Santa María de Magdalena and the white igloo-shaped crypt in which lie, in a glass case, the bones of the town's founding father, Father Eusebio Kino. When Angie sets out from Tucson, with Glenda and Jillian, she doesn't realize that it's the Festival of San Francisco Xavier, a time when people make pilgrimages to Magdalena, walking sometimes one hundred miles or more as they have done for years, centuries, maybe, and she wonders if their devotion has thus charged the ions in the air and if maybe that's how Juana of God is able to perform her miracles.

Do you have to believe in God or Christ, she wonders, for Juana to cure you? She thinks not. After all, that handsome doctor didn't seem to be religious. Even though his wound was exactly where Christ's was, he didn't say anything about God, not God the Father, not God the Son, nor God the Holy Ghost. Neither did Oprah. She didn't even ask the obvious Oprah questions.

Angie is a more-than-lapsed Catholic, but even she could see it: looking at that wound was like looking at the stigmata and saying nothing. Curious. Jesus as the elephant in the room. Angie has heard of cathedrals in Mexico where the stone floors have grooves worn in them from people crawling on their knees to the altar. Even if you don't believe in God, she thinks, even if you don't believe in Jesus as the Son of God, as the Lamb of God, who takes away the sins of the world, there must be something to believe in—even if it's only the faith of others. But for now, she just drives carefully, hoping that no pedestrian or pilgrim will decide to test God by stepping in front of her car.

3

They come into the café every morning for desayuno, the woman with her hair as if it is on fire, la rubia in the wheelchair, and the girl who does not talk. They did not know it was the festival and so the woman, she was very upset at the streets full of people. She had hoped, she said, for "más cálmate," by which I think she was not telling me "more you calm down" but saying instead that she wished the town was more quiet, not so noisy with the bands and the dancing in the streets. So I set a table aside for them in the corner and every morning, it's the same thing. La rubia in the wheelchair gets a quesadilla because no matter how much her hand shakes, she can bring it to her mouth. The mother of the girl, she gets huevos rancheros, and the girl, when she points to tacos de lengua on the menu, the mother shrugs and says, á ella le gusta la carne. Every morning. Evidently the mother does not see the irony that we see—those of us busy in the kitchen—a girl who cannot speak eating lengua.

"Tell me," the mother of the girl says to me on the third morning, "what do you know of this Juana of God? And why is it we have to wait so long for an appointment?"

Of course, it is a coincidence for right at that moment, Juana y su marido Nardo are sitting at their table, which is set aside for them in the other corner of the restaurant. But I say nothing. Because. Who knows if Juana wants to see them?

"All I know," I say, "is that Juana has taken away my tooth aches. With one touch of her fingers, she lifts away the pain. She has even taken away the dreams of my teeth crumbling in my mouth. Perhaps that is worth waiting for."

The mother tilts her head as though considering this and just then the silent girl lifts her face and I know she recognizes Juana of God—who could forget her?—the thick eyebrows that meet in a line like Frida's, the snow white hair piled high on her head, the huge hoop earrings, the heavy turquoise rings on her fingers and the dozens of jangling bracelets. Juana is a striking woman. With her full breasts and haunches, she looks like one of those goddesses before la virgen ever showed herself to Juan Diego.

Right now, Juana is eating a breakfast of pastries that I make especially for her in the old French way, butter, crema, eggs, all the things she is not supposed to have because of her heart disease. It is like the painter whose house needs painting, the healer who needs a cure. What can I say?

When I go over to her table to tell her that she has visitors, she pats the chair next to her. "Sientate, Jorge. Let me tell you what those American doctors did to me. They pumped my veins full of radio-activity and I could feel myself begin to glow. All through my veins, up my right arm, into my armpit, into my lungs and heart, even into my brain, I could feel it. The warmth like scorpion venom. It was moving all through me, down into my legs, up into my other arm, lighting me up like thousands of stars."

"And so what did they say?"

"Nada," Nardo says, "nada que ya no sabemos."

"Pfft!" Juana waves her hand. "But as if that is not bad enough! They make you run on this treadmill as if you are a rat, a rat with wires all taped to you. You are full of their poison and you have wires taped to you and they watch the computer as you run. They do not watch you. You could fall off and hit your head and die and they would not notice until their computer told them to look. And then, while you are running as fast as you can, they pump still more poison into you and it burns like hell and no matter if you say it burns, they do not listen. All of this just so they can see inside you because, without their machines and their poisons, they cannot see inside."

The mother rises and begins to push la rubia towards the door and right then Juana's little Chihuahua begins to growl deep in his throat.

"Pay attention to the dog!" Nardo warns them. "He bites!"

But the silent girl, she comes over to our table and puts her hand on Juana's shoulder and Junie, I swear, he stops growling. He does not bite. It's the only time he has ever let a stranger touch Juana of God.

"Ah," Juana belches, a deep one, from her whole body. She studies the girl's serious face. "You have a gift, Mi'ja. That was just what I needed."

4

White is not in the palette of Jillian's wardrobe. Nor is it in her mother's nor in Glenda's, but after much grumbling about the commercialism of the Juana of God enterprise and how it supports the whole god-damned town, her mother buys peasant blouses for the three of them from a store on the Plaza Monumental. They are thin white cotton with bright embroidered flowers all along the top and the edges of the sleeves. On Glenda's, even the flowers are white since she is the patient, which makes Jillian think she is like a nun or a bride or an angel. Even The Casa, which is what the people call Juana of God's hacienda, is white. White walls, white floors, white domed roof, white ceilings, white curtains. Has color been erased? Have they died and gone to a bland heaven? These questions enter Jillian's mind.

In the courtyard of The Casa Blanca, as Jillian now thinks of it, rows and rows of white plastic lawn chairs filled with rows and rows of supplicants dressed in white clothing. Jillian and her mother wheel Glenda in and take two chairs on the aisle next to her. A red flash of the wings of a cardinal, green leaves of huge plants sway in terra cotta pots, fronds of the palm trees above them rustle. These are the only splashes of color. Junie, the Chihuahua, struts across the stage. And then Juana appears in a white pantsuit and is standing in the center of the stage where the visible healing takes place, where she gets inhabited by a saint or by an old German doctor or by Florence Nightingale, maybe, or by Oswaldo Cruz, or maybe by several entities in succession, depending on what the patients need. There is the visible healing where people go up on to the stage and get healed because the entity enters Juana of God and she goes into a trance and the entity operates. Not Juana. Juana does not operate for, as even she will tell you, she has no medical training and, besides, as her assistants will tell you, the sight of blood makes her swoon—Jillian knows this from watching Oprah—and then there is the *in*visible healing which happens when people in the audience sit and quietly focus on their own inner need for healing and then the spirit entities move among them and even inside of them and leave invisible sutures.

Jillian, of course, can't wait to see blood spurting from people's noses or to see the part where Juana sticks her hand inside someone's body, right through the skin!

But, until then: all around Jillian, the rising hum of everyone's desires for wholeness and, she has to say, some of their desires are a little crass. Even her mother's. Since she is closest to Jillian, Jillian can hear her mother's desire for money. Her mother believes that if only she could win the lottery, she would have enough money to take care of everything else herself. She wouldn't need Juana of God or even God, although, as a more-than-lapsed Catholic, she doesn't dare think this for more than one nanosecond. (Of course, she needs God.) But she *could*. Take care of everything. The Lord helps those who help themselves, after all. If she had money, she could quit her job and take care of Glenda and take care of her mother and Jillian and even Stevie Jr., whom they've had to leave behind with her mother. (Poor Stevie Jr., Jillian suddenly thinks, imagining her fierce grandmother yanking the remote out of Stevie Jr.'s hand so she can watch *Wheel! of! Fortune!*) Meanwhile her mother is almost in a frenzy of anxiety, revising her monetary needs up and up and up, more and more and more zeroes, because she'll need help, won't she? For years. No, for decades. What with her mother's declining health as well as Glenda's, she'll need two Marisols, at least, and if she takes in two Marisols, then she'll have to take in Marisol One's granddaughter, Bella, and probably another Bella for the other Marisol, for she doesn't want to exploit anyone, and she'll need a bigger house for all of them to live together and she'll have to put the Bellas through college as well as Stevie Jr. and Jillian. And Stevie Jr. will probably want to go to graduate school, for he is one smart cookie, and Jillian, if Jillian wants to go to Art School, Angie is determined that she will. Why, oh why, had she bought the white blouses? They didn't really need them, did they, to come here? And why did she buy that expensive face lotion and that expensive wine the other night and why had she put the airline tickets on her card instead of letting her mother pay for them?

And what if she has to sell the house to take care of Glenda? The more Angie thinks about everyone who needs her and how little money she has saved and how much she wastes—one of her cards is at 19.99%!—and how little she earns from her job and how she's run out of sick leave and vacation time—although everyone tells her she should be thankful she even had that!—and how the cost of medical care is going up and Glenda's insurance is running out—thank God, her mother has Tri-Care for life but even that doesn't cover long-term care—and how little Jillian's father Bobby sends and how Steve Sr. sends nothing, a big fat zilch, for Stevie Jr., the more and more oppressed she feels and the more and more money she thinks she needs and the more she wishes she just had something simple wrong with her, even a tumor, say, so that Juana of God could just shove something up her nose and cure it once and for all. Yes, if her money woes could be over, if she could quit the nightly tossing and turning that started as soon as she heard about Glenda's accident, she would let someone shove knitting needles up her nose. She would. She would let someone stab her in the stomach and give her the stigmata. Let the bleeding begin!

At this, Jillian takes her mother's hand and strokes it. She presses her other hand against her mother's cheek. Shhh, Jillian thinks to her mother, and to all the others whose needs are rising in them, whose knots of anxiety are twisting and twisting. Does Juana of God hear them, too? She wonders.

5

El perrito, nightmare of my existence, the way he nips at my heels. If he were a bigger dog, he would be dead already. He barks, and it is a signal that Juana is about to begin. Juana, whose Casa I have been cleaning. ¿Juana es de Díos? No sé. Anything is possible, pues, but when you clean a person's toilet, you know things about her no one else should know. Juana is of the flesh and God is ineffable. Of this, I have no doubt. Perhaps God works through her in the way He works through all of us. An act of kindness here, you give money there, a crust of bread, a tortilla, whatever you can because the beggar at your door may be the Savior—¿quién sabe?—who knows, you never know—but does this mean Juana is any closer to God than the rest of us? Je ne sais pas! as the French would say.

She is a curandera, okay, of this I am sure—and a good one, maybe, one hopes she does no harm—it's just that she's found her market and a curandera, she is not supposed to have a market. She is supposed to give her gifts freely for they came to her freely—but such is the free market system and its power to corrupt. After years of living en el otro lado, of this I can testify. ¡Ay, Díos mío! Los norteamericanos, they are the only ones in the world who think that God proves Himself by granting wishes and giving prosperity.

And so Junie barks and so I see them, my norteamericanos, Angie and Glenda and Jillian. They are sitting a few rows in front of me. At first, my heart skips a beat for I am hoping and also not hoping that they have brought my Bella, mi nieta, who was left behind in the States when I got deported. Oh, mi vida. I wonder how she is doing without me and if she knows I am cleaning baños as fast as I can to get back to her, working my way north, for even in México there are those who don't like to clean their own bathrooms.

When Angie stands up and pushes her sister forward, up the ramp, on to the stage, Jillian, pobrecita, is left by herself and so I move up and sit next to her. She is a strange one, I know, but sweet. She touches my hand without even looking at me, as if she were expecting me, Marisol, to come and sit next to her, as if to say "Hi!" She is looking at the dog as if she expects him to change into a much larger being, a mythical creature. This is something I also expect of him and so I remind him, often, to keep him in his place, that my ancestors ate his ancestors. You exist only because your ancestors were raised for food, I tell him, and then he slinks away like the little hairless dog that he is.

On stage, Juana has gone into one of her trances and the voice that comes out of her mouth, y eso es la verdad, I swear, is the voice of a very old man who is stuck in a tunnel. It is not a voice I have heard before. It is speaking a language other than Spanish or English or French, and I look down and the girl, Jillian, is drawing in a notebook and in the drawing, there is a small creature with wings and with the face of el perrito, Junie. El perrito, he is pierced with small arrows and his bug-eyes roll up in his head like the eyes of a saint. And now she is drawing, I see it: Juana holding out her hand for the knife and, around Juana, like a shadow, the larger shape of a man, a man in old-fashioned clothing. And now another shadow and now another, until all over the page there are shadows, what is left of those who have gone before us, maybe, gathered there on the stage hearing our sad prayers. And so I think, maybe these norteamericanos are on to something. Maybe we, los pobres, are behind the times, thinking we're supposed to serve God and not the other way around.

Entonces. ¿Quién sabe? Maybe God will grant our wishes. Can it hurt to try? And so I do, I try, and even as I try, I know, I can feel it, there is a difference between praying and wishing, because with praying, your whole soul rises and expands and becomes filled with light, but with wishing, it is only half of your soul, not enough light to share with others. I can feel part of my heart holding back and this, I know, is my own lack. Me falta not faith in God but the belief that prayers are for wishing. This is a lack that is in me and not God's fault. Still, I try to wish, like the others seated around me, and I wish not to be Mexican.

I want to be cured of being Mexican? Oh, no, that is not what I intend. Soy una méxicana, siempre. By this I mean I want to go back to where is my home now, the area of the bay, San Francisco. I want a claim to my own life. I want to be free to belong where I belong. My blood will always be here in this soil, but the heart that pumps my blood is in el otro lado, with my nieta Bella, where I am needed. Here, I will come back here to die.

6

Even before Marisol sits next to her, Jillian has been drawing what she sees. She has drawn a brown cloud coming out of the dog's mouth like a puff of earthy dust or smoke and, as it materialized, it became a man in a brown suit, and then another cloud floated forward and it was a woman in a long black gown and then another and another and another, too many for Jillian to draw all at once. Then Junie, the dog, sprouted wings and then arrows pierced him as if he were a small deer being hunted by invisible archers, and when his eyes rolled back in his head, the head of Juana of God snapped back and snapped forward and when she opened her mouth, a gravelly voice, the voice of an old man, came out. The voice said unters messen kommen and because Jillian, in her few moments of omniscience when she was being born, was granted a limited vocabulary in many languages—a particularly ironic gift since she would never be able to speak any of them—she understood that the voice was saying something about undergoing the knife and it must have been true because when Juana of God held out her hand—although she was no longer all there and so to say she held out her hand seems to imply a volition that she did not, in actuality, have—an assistant, who was also dressed all in white, slapped a dinner knife in her palm. Slapped, as if she needed to be sure that Juana could feel it.

Just then, as Marisol sits next to her, Jillian watches as Juana of God steps up to a man with a goatee, the first supplicant, and he puts both of his hands over his heart, and Juana is mumbling something, perhaps praying, Jillian thinks, although she is now drawing so quickly, all of her consciousness focused on her hand moving across the page, that she isn't really paying attention to sound. All is vision. Juana has stretched the man's eyelids apart and she has begun to scrape his eyeball with the dinner knife. The man seems to feel no pain. He doesn't say a word, he doesn't lift his hands from his chest, he doesn't even seem to resist by pulling his head back. Jillian can see a glowing red spot on the man's left lung, it is glowing through his skin, and so she wonders *why the eyeball when he has a growth on his lung?* But now Juana of God is moving towards her mother and her aunt.

Later, much later, Jillian will wonder why it did not surprise her when Juana of God went directly to her mother, as if Angie were the patient and not Glenda but, of course, because Juana was in a trance, not seeing the world as it existed in front of her eyes but seeing, instead, some version of it painted inside her own mind, Juana of God moved toward Angie and she put her hand on Angie's shoulder and Angie put her hands over her heart, as if she were, indeed, the supplicant, the person who was in need of healing. The voice that came out of Juana of God's mouth this time was in an ancient language, so ancient that none of her assistants understood her. It was a language of trees growing or of magma from deep in the earth or of ancient water, a language without words, but Juana seemed to understand it and Jillian, as she drew, understood it in her muscles and bones for she could draw so quickly as if she were drawing a movie, as if the drawing was causing the events to happen and not merely recording them.

Juana of God lifted Angie's shirt and there was Angie's smooth white stomach with one dark mole right below her left breast and Juana plunged her hand into Angie's stomach, right through the skin, no need for a knife, no need for an incision. Even the assistants gasped, even the shadows on the stage gasped, and the spirits who were moving among the supplicants seated for invisible healing, they all gasped, and Juana drew out of Angie's stomach a large black stone, like a river stone, pure black, heavy, worn smooth by millennia and millennia of water running over it, and she handed the stone to Glenda who took it in her hands and pressed it to her cheek. Juana pulled stone after stone out of Angie's stomach until there were seven stones and, after each stone, she handed it to Glenda and Glenda held it first to her cheek and then cradled it in her lap. No one could believe that seven such large stones had been housed in such a thin body. After the last stone, Juana of God seemed to look at her own hand, for she held it to the sky and turned it back and forth, and then she waved her hand over Angie's stomach and the skin was smooth, healed, as if it had never been broken.

Jillian continues to draw and, in her drawing, her mother floats up above the stage, she seems very happy, and Jillian draws a large house below her and, in the house, she draws her grandmother and Stevie Jr. watching TV. She draws Bella knocking at the front door. She draws the handsome American doctor, the one from the Ivy Leagues who was on Oprah. He comes up on the stage to help Angie with Glenda. He loves the smooth stones, holds them to his own cheek, one by one, and then he takes Glenda's face in his hands and she whispers—what, Jillian cannot hear for her head is bent over her drawing—but they are the first words Glenda has uttered since her accident and, although Jillian does not believe in fairy tales, she knows what kind of woman her aunt is, a woman who is only happy when she is with a man, and so Jillian draws her floating up out of the chair and she and the doctor are flying slant-wise over the stage as if they are the bride and groom in the painting by Chagall. They have left the stones that burdened Angie below. The stones are below in the wheelchair. Angie begins to sing, a song like a lullaby and everyone, including the spirits, including Juana of God, including Junie, the channeling Chihuahua, feel as if someone invisible is cradling them. Sutures, visible and invisible, anywhere within fifty miles, melt and leave no marks.

7

Jillian draws a sunny day for their departure. When they pack up the car, they will leave the stones behind because now that the doctor and Marisol are traveling with them, there is no room for the stones and, besides, Juana of God wants to use them in her herb garden. She will swap them for payment because she is sure they will help her grow the most marvelous herbs. She is sad to see the doctor go, primarily because he was such good publicity, but c'est la vie, que será será, and all that. Even Junie, for all his growling at Marisol, wishes her the best, hopes she won't be deposited again in the middle of the burning desert.

Goodbye, he barks. Goodbye! Good Luck!

Marisol, remembering when he bit her finger, gives him the evil eye, but Jillian waves. Junie, she knows, contains multitudes and so it is not surprising that he's a little schizophrenic.

As they approach the border, Jillian feels overwhelmed with the lines and lines of cars, their hulking bodies, their exhaust rising in gray ghost clouds. Likewise, she is overwhelmed by the little girls wilting like paper flowers, *chicle for sale* melting in the palms of their hands, and the grubby boys who clamor at the windows and climb on the hoods of cars, waving their spray bottles and squeegees.

Not to mention: on the periphery of her vision, the shadows of teenagers on this side who were shot for throwing rocks at the Border Patrol on that side, or who were shot for trying to climb the fence back into this country, or who were shot as they walked along a street on this side, across from the wall, head down, eyes averted, hunched shoulders. Jose Antonio Elena Rodriguez. Seven bullets in the back, that's how the corrido will go. One day, there should be a song remembering, Jillian thinks.

She looks down at her drawing. She hopes the guards won't notice Marisol—Marisol, who at this moment, is doing her best to vanish and so is becoming thinner and thinner to the point of near translucence, almost melting into the upholstery between Jillian and her mother. Jillian scoots closer as if to hide her. She hopes the guards will be too mesmerized by her mother's singing and too busy looking at the lovebirds in the backseat and at the light that emanates from the car itself to notice Marisol.

The light, which is the light of concentrated prayers, will blind them, Jillian decides. It will be a laser-beam light, a light so bright that the car can rise above all the other cars and float over the border in a bubble—this is how Jillian draws the car—in a blue bubble with tongues of light all around, just like la virgen of Guadalupe in those paintings on velvet. For it is true, la virgen can go anywhere. Borders never stop her. Maybe, Jillian thinks, maybe Marisol's escape will count as the miracle they've been hoping for.

Jillian Speaks

*In which Jillian encounters her long-lost father, then loses him
again, and thus learns to speak, in a manner of speaking.*

1

Bobby Guzmán, Angie O'Malley thinks when she opens the door
and sees the long-lost love of her life. That's all she thinks. That's
it. Bobby Guzmán. His name. She doesn't think, Bobby Guzmán,
where have you been? She doesn't think, Bobby Guzmán, where the
hell is my back-child support? No, she just registers the fact of him
in the flesh, pure and simple, but this is because, ever since Juana
of God lifted the seven black river stones out of her belly, she has
felt much lighter. All anxiety and resentment have fallen away. She
is calm. She knows all is as it should be. Qué será será and all that.

Besides, and it must be said, even at forty-five, Bobby Guzmán
is one good-looking guy, what with that thick black hair and those
white teeth, not to mention his broad shoulders and the way his
shirt sleeves just reveal his biceps and how they are round and firm
and just a little paler than the rest of his skin. *Oh*, Angie thinks,
Bobby. It's as if the intervening years have been erased, as if all sadness has fallen away, as if all is forgiven. Bobby. She suddenly feels
how lonely she's been.

"My liver is as bumpy as a toad."

That is the first thing he tells her.

He wants her to know he isn't making any promises? Were it not for his liver, he would not be standing on her doorstep? But really? Not: I love you. Not: I'm sorry. Not: Can you forgive me? Not even: I've missed you—and oh, and by the way, the surgeon says my liver is as bumpy as a toad.

The last time she'd seen him, it had been at a party. A few years ago. He was with another woman, walking up the stairs. To the bedroom? He had that shy look of pleasure on his face and she'd felt this long- ing, this regret, that she was not the woman on the stairs, would not be the woman in the bed. And the woman had looked so willing to give herself over completely to him, which was something Angie had never been able to do. Not fully. Angie was not one who surrendered, even in love-making. There was always at least a tiny bit of herself she held back.

She knows she's not what anyone would call a generous person, a forgiving person. Had she found fault with things that now would strike her as inconsequential? Yes. She'd held grudges: also true. She *had* changed her name, and Jillian's, from Guzmán back to O'Malley just to spite him. (For instance.) (How white of you, he'd said.) So she knows it must be hard for him to come back. If indeed he is back.

But: My liver is as bumpy as a toad? That's what he'd said. All he'd said.

And when she doesn't respond?

"Can I come in?"

Then he touches her. A pang goes from her throat to the root of her, a spasm twisting through her heart and gut. It's a warning, maybe.

She leads him into the living room where Glenda, in a wheel-chair, is reading from a children's book as her boyfriend slides his finger under the huge print. Her mother's watching golf on the TV. Of course, she looks up long enough to give Bobby a solid glare, just like in the old days. Jillian's sitting at the dining room table with Stevie Jr. and Bella. They're all doing their homework. Jillian looks up, but then just turns back to her book.

Angie can see the dismay on Bobby's face. Her knees go weak with the sorrow of it. Things have changed. But what did he expect?

"Yes," she says, "they all live here. Don't ask."

She takes a breath. She doesn't need any more stones in her belly, no more knots around her heart. Think about it, she tells herself, when someone's in trouble and they turn to you, that means something, doesn't it? It certainly means they feel loved *by* you. They trust you. Or at least there's a bond that hasn't been broken.

2

When Jillian's dad, Bobby, talked about the TCE that made his liver bumpy, she saw it as a huge darkness spreading underneath the ground. She saw men in uniforms cleaning airplanes and airplane parts and then pouring the used solvent into barrels, loading the barrels into beds of trucks like army trucks with canvasses over the back, like in old movies about World War II, although these trucks had lots of barrels inside of them and inside of the barrels, this solvent was bubbling and eating away at the metal. The men had on gloves, they had to be very careful, and they unloaded the barrels from the trucks and opened them with screwdrivers and dumped the liquid into ponds, ponds that were not lined with cement or lead or anything, and so it was as if they were pouring the solvent right into the dirt. If the dirt of the ground had been alive like an organism instead of only alive with organisms, if it had been skin instead of only the surface of the earth, it would have sizzled and shriveled and screamed. Jillian was sure of this. Instead, only the organisms in it sizzled and shriveled and died. They did not scream for the earth does not scream, and the liquid seeped down deeper and deeper, a dark stain spreading underneath the ground, seeping deep into the sand in the washes, into the water in the pools beneath the skin of the earth, spreading wide beneath creosote bushes, beneath Palo Verde trees and mesquite, into snake holes and rabbit holes and the dens of pack rats and the cute little squirrels, Juancitos, her father called them, beneath the prickly pear and ocotillo and tender grasses and brittlebush, beneath the houses people lived in, beneath their horse corrals and chicken coops, beneath vegetable gardens and citrus trees, beneath swimming pools and schools and parks and playgrounds and even hospitals. If your soul flew up into the sky at night, up near the stars, it would be able to see the darkness spreading beneath the skin of the earth and if it rained, as if to wash it all away, it only washed it deeper into the sands and the stones and the ancient waters below the dry surface of the desert.

This, her father was sure, was why he was sick. Sure, he had drunk a few beers in his life, he would admit that, but he had also drunk that water when he was a child. He had bathed in it and poured it over his head with a garden hose on hot summer days and when he went to the swimming pool, he had leaped into it with his friends, his friends who were also growing bumps on their livers and kidneys or tumors in their brains or testicles, or getting diseases of the blood, who were also dying or dead. And not only were his friends dying but their parents were dead, not to mention their aunts and uncles, their brothers and sisters, their wives and children, which is why he was so glad, in retrospect, that he'd left Jillian behind after the divorce and had not taken her with him to the south side of town where all the Mexicans and Indians lived, where there were now red lines around housing developments and where the clean-up, although it had begun years ago, was too late for him, too late for so many.

When he was a kid, he told Jillian, the water had effervesced right from the faucet, a rainbow in your glass.

3

La guera, Angie, when I knocked at her door, she was surprised to see me. After all, it's not every day that Juana of God shows up on your doorstep. But I wanted to check in on her and her sister Glenda and the girl who does not speak (although she could if she wanted or so the spirits tell me), and we'd been at the hospital, Nardo and Junie and me, and we needed a place to rest before making the trek back to Magdalena. La Angie, she seemed happier now that her house was full of people and now that her novio was home. And that is what the nuns always taught me: if you have only a crust of bread, better to share than to keep it all to yourself. What you give, it will come back.

But this novio, this Bobby, he was not well. Even Nardo could see it. Even little Junie. We had come for my yearly torture with the cardiologist and, again, el doctor had filled my veins with poison and taped his wires to my chest and made me run on a treadmill, faster and faster. *¡Juanita, can't you go any faster?* And he looked at his computer to see inside me, mi corazón, pumping and pumping on his screen, about to explode if you ask me but, of course, he never asks me. *¡Juanita,* he told me, *faster!* He knows nothing of Juana of God, and that is just as well, but no one has called me Juanita since I was a niña at the orphanage in the hills of Magdalena and so it made me feel as if I would get a swat on my knuckles and so siempre I try to do as he says.

"Tell me," I said to this Bobby, who is muy guapo, I must say, la guera, she has good taste in men. "Tell me about this surgery."

We were sitting at the dining room table, Nardo and Bobby and Angie and me, drinking coffee, and Marisol brought out some almond scones with dried cherries and white chocolate and I was thinking about what el doctor would say about that when Junie started growling and, for a Chihuahua, I have to say, he has quite a deep voice. Even though he and Marisol are ancient enemies, you would think they could have come to some sort of agreement by now, but No.

"Watch it," she told him, "or you'll be an hors d'oeuvre."

And did he stop? No, he nipped at her ankles, he wouldn't back down, and so I had to pick him up and, still, safe in my lap, he growled.

"He's been falling over a lot," Nardo told Marisol as if that would soften her heart. "It's like he has a seizure or something. Clunk, over he goes, and then he gets up a few minutes later as if nothing happened."

Marisol just shrugged and put a bowl of crema on the table. "Maybe it's the spirits in him," she said. "Están cansados."

Espíritu santo, I was thinking. Even God must get tired these days.

Bobby was saying that there was a growth on his liver and they biopsied it with a long needle. Malignant. Then they went in and took it out and it was much bigger than they expected. And it had spread. Like wildfire. More tumors.

"They stuck a needle in it?" Nardo asked.

"They woke it up," I said.

"That's what I thought," Bobby said. "They pissed it off."

"Es la verdad," I said, "those procedures, como se dice, invasive, I don't believe in them."

Marisol rolled her eyes. "This from la mujer who scrapes the eyeballs de los enfermos with a kitchen knife?"

Angie shook her head at Bobby. "And who plunged her hand into my gut and pulled out seven stones. Without anesthesia. No stitches needed."

"If I did that," I said, "it escapes me."

I felt a little woozy just imagining it.

"It was the spirits," Nardo said, patting my hand. "She doesn't even like the sight of blood."

"Or the thought of pain," I said.

"I didn't feel a thing," Angie shrugged.

"This cancer you have," I asked Bobby, "it is from the poison they poured into the ground? No? The Air Force, I think."

"For years," he said. "Since 1952."

"I've seen so many people sick from that, so many. They come down to la casa to be healed. Pero a veces the cancer is muy fuerte. No hay nada que hacer."

"That's what every doctor tells me: *I have done everything I can.*"

"My prima, Marta," Marisol broke in, "she died from it. It was the lymphoma, it went straight to her brain. One day she was loca, two months later, dead. Only forty years old and with three kids. If she'd stayed in Cananea, she'd still be alive."

I waved my hand in the air and the rings and the bracelets made a music to gather everyone's attention. "Los pobres," I said. "They may as well be los desaparecidos. No one sees them. So what does it matter which side they live on, north or south? No one has a voice. Nadie."

And then Bobby, he's a smart one, he went on about how the poison sinks to the bottom of the wells, to water that is millions of years old, maybe, and they would have to pump it all out and filter it somehow, tu sabes, which is muy muy caro, and so they shut down the wells. "But do you think it stays put? It's liquid! ¡Que pendejos!"

I put Junie down on the floor and he whimpered. "Come over here with me, Bobby," I said because, and this is what I was thinking, we can do nothing about the past, and our anger, maybe it feeds the cancer. Puede ser. "Now lie down on the couch and close your eyes. Take a deep breath."

I was trying to draw the spirits to me, but I was so tired, and Junie had been falling over lately, es la verdad, sometimes several times a day. This channeling is not an easy business, no matter what anyone says. But I gathered myself, I opened myself to God or whoever else might be listening, whatever angel, and of course Bobby has his own angels all around him. I rubbed my hands together, warming my palms, and then I laid my hands on him, on his liver and all around it. He was very sick. I called them to help me. I felt their warmth and power, but I knew maybe all I could hope for was to take away the pain. I prayed anyways. I filled my heart with their prayers and my own, and we stayed like that for a while, but none of the doctor spirits entered me. Not one. I always feel like such a failure when this happens, but what can you do?

This I know: there are times when there is no hope for what will happen in this world, where what people have set into motion, the spirits cannot reverse. Qúe será será, no matter how strong the will. All we can do then is accept the truth for in acceptance there is, sometimes, something as great as peace. Maybe it is faith. ¿Quien sabe? I don't know. No one knows. All this, I said to him in my thoughts and I know he heard me. We were all quiet, hushed, our hearts on hold, we were trying to pray even though we knew, we all knew, and it was a sad thing. The light was draining from the room. We heard the voices of the children coming home from school, a plane overhead.

"Mi'jo," I said, because I did feel a great love for him, "you have to make a truce with this thing. *Live and let live.* Every night, you tell it this: you will let it live inside you if it will let you live."

4

All the way down to her tata's house, all the way down South 12th Ave., Jillian's eyes were filled with color, bright yellow and pink and blue storefronts. ¡Mariscos! ¡Panaderia! ¡Carniceria! ¡Raspados! Her dad stopped at Dos Hermanos to get menudo and pan birrote and while he was inside the store, she started drawing the storefronts with their big black letters and the wrought iron over the windows. Somehow, because it was a particular gift of hers, she could see different eras superimposed over one another as if time were not linear but instead a palimpsest, one layer on top of another, and so she could also see how it had all looked back when her dad was young, the round green buses belching their black fumes and the boarded-up windows on the stores and houses and old cars and so many people walking, whole families, and then, when they turned on the side-streets, she saw everyone who used to live there. It was literally a ghost town, all the people who had died from the TCE rose up as soon as they turned the corner. As if to give a shout out to her dad, they came out to the curbs and waved as he and Jillian drove down the street. It was as if the people who had gone before wanted to tell him they were waiting, and he wouldn't be alone when he left this world.

Of course, there were also people who had taken their places, who walked on the ground they had risen out of, who had moved into their houses and had only a slight sensation of cold air on occasion or a glimpse in their peripheral vision, who parked their big trucks in the driveways and on the streets, the stereos blaring Mexican music and rap, the little kids weaving in and out on their bikes, the dogs yipping and the meat sizzling on the barbeques. Jillian drew them all, the living and the dead, the palm trees and the leafy green trees, the bright bougainvillea and hollyhocks and oleander, the saints in their grottos as if the people still lived in Mexico. She half-expected to see parrots or other tropical birds and so she drew them, too, swooping above the gray ghosts.

When her tata opened the door, she saw that her dad looked just like his dad except his dad was old. He had white hair and lots of wrinkles, a bigger nose and very long ears, and Jillian knew, suddenly, in a flash of heat to her heart, that her father would never get that old. She felt the sudden shadow of future sorrow as it fell over all three of them.

Half in English and half in Spanish, her dad and her tata started talking, a river of language she could follow because fortunately when she was born, even though she wasn't given the gift of gab, the universe had downloaded some rudimentary Spanish into her brain. Listening to her dad talk this way, seeing her tata, she suddenly remembered her dad from when she was little, how his tee shirts used to smell like a dusty sun with a little Old Spice and how she used to wrap her dolls in them. She remembered that he loved cartoons on the TV and when he'd come home from work, they'd sit on the floor and eat cold cereal at the coffee table and watch Roadrunner and Coyote, Yosemite Sam, those old school ones, and even the neighborhood kids would come over and knock on the door and her dad would pour bowls of cereal for them, too, and her dad would laugh and laugh like he was still a kid himself. He didn't care if they drank up all the milk and ate up all the cereal and, when her mom complained about it, he'd say, okay, I'll give them mine. Or, when have I ever let you go hungry?

Why was she remembering all this now, she wondered. And why, now that he was here, did she suddenly miss him? She suddenly missed all those years he'd been gone. She was ravenous, not for his attention, exactly, but just to be near him, in proximity, as if she could soak him up and make up for lost time. And truth be told, she was a little angry at him. And at her mom. She remembered echoes of their arguments, not the words, just the sharp discordant notes that had started at breakfast and seemed to never stop, her mother talking talking talking, always talking, an undertow drowning her father, a riptide sweeping him away, driving him to drink is what he said, so it wasn't like he was blameless. He was wrong, too. But why hadn't they been able to overcome those problems for her? Was it so much to ask? She could see herself in the backseat of the car one summer night, words zinging like arrows until she, Jillian, had wished she were deaf as well as mute, until she'd shoved her head under her pillow, until she couldn't breathe, until the backseat of the car felt like a dark airless oven.

One time when her mother was driving, her father had jumped out at a stop sign and disappeared into the night. What was that all about? Someone's had too much to drink, her mother said, and they left him behind.

But. Whatever. Jillian told herself that was all in the past now, gone, nothing anyone could do about it, and so she started to worry about future lost time instead of past lost time because she could see inside her dad and something was growing there that shouldn't be. It gave her a scary feeling, like there are things you know will happen, darkness, pain, and you can't stop them from coming. Just like the darkness had spread beneath the ground, seeping into rivulets between stones, reaching out its tentacles, now it was doing the same thing inside him, pooling in his liver, spreading through his veins, changing his cells.

Her dad and her tata, their talking went back and forth between languages often in the middle of a sentence, and in this way, her father was breaking the bad news about his bumpy liver to his dad, who had to sit down when he heard it. It knocked him right off his feet and would have in any language, Jillian supposed, since at one time, a long time ago, before she was ever born, her tata had held her dad in his arms and maybe even had changed his diaper, although Jillian doubted it if only because her mother always said, That Bobby! He never even changed a diaper!

Her tata said the woman next door had lost three of her five children. And Juan. Did her dad remember him? He'd worked on the roofs with her tata, he was one of the first to get the cancer, and he'd been smart enough to get in on the lawsuit.

"But now," her tata rubbed his fingers and thumb together, "no one else will ever see a dime."

"Nope," her dad said. "Nada."

"Those pinche lawyers, they took it all."

Her dad nodded. They were both quiet for a while, eating their menudo. Although they were no longer speaking aloud, she could still hear them. Her father was thinking about how he wouldn't be able to leave anything for her, how he'd had to sell his house even though he'd had insurance, how his medical bills had taken up everything he'd saved, and now there was no time to earn more. And her tata, he was just sad. He had been orphaned as a child in Mexico, had to flee federales, cross the border by himself, and so he didn't expect justice, not in this life, not for himself, but he had expected something better for his son. Jillian began to draw her dad and she wondered, if she drew him getting well, if she believed he would get well, would that work?

5

¡Ay, ay, ay, Lois, la viejita! She still insists on calling me María, even though everyone knows my name is Marisol—even Glenda, who, as we all know, has a problem with her memories. I sometimes wonder what would happen if I refused to answer Lois and why, after all these years, has it started to bother me?

"You know what it is, Marisol," Angie me dije, "it's because you and me, we're the ones doing all the work around here."

Y por supuesto, tiene razón. I was like a nurse what with Glenda still recovering from her motorcycle accident and Lois who had, as even she would say, old-timer's disease. More and more demented every day.

"Two head cases," Angie said. "If we left them to their own devices, they'd burn the place down."

And now Bobby, pobrecito. I knew a man, he had a bad liver, and his stomach got as round and hard as a melón and he went loco, puro loco, and his wife, she had to lock him in his room and hammer boards over the windows so he wouldn't escape the house and then they had to come and tie him up and take him away. I didn't want Bella to see such a sad thing, and I hoped it would not come to pass.

But what can I say? If I had to take care of three people whose minds were lost, I would ask Angie for more. Although, Glenda, she needs less help every day. She can talk again. Sometimes, no one understands what she says, es la verdad, one word jumps in and takes the place of another. I put my ship in my apple, she says. Or I've lost my Alaska. I've lost my Alaska? Ensalada de las palabras, that novio of hers, Jack, calls it. But she can use el baño again, sin ayuda, gracias a Dios, since that was my job.

Bobby and Jack, after Jack gets Glenda to bed, they talk way late into the night even without drinking beers. The other night they were talking about ancient water. ¡El agua viejo! Whoever heard of such a thing, but I heard Bobby saying about how, when you go down a mile and a half, the water is millions of years old.

"The next war is going to be over water," Jack said.

"No shit," Bobby said. "Forget about oil."

Just then, la niña, Jillian, she wandered out from her room. Her eyes were wide open and she sat down next to Bobby and put her head on his shoulder and then closed her eyes again.

"No wonder they didn't worry about TCE," Bobby said. "They figured, who knows, 50 deaths per 1,000 people. Or whatever. A calculated risk. And they needed to clean their planes and make their bombs."

"Collateral damage," Jack said.

"We were just Mexicans."

"What I don't get, though," Jack said, "is if you guys saw rainbows in the water, why didn't you do something about it?"

Bobby sighed. "We did. We called. It was a new house, well. They said it was the pipes and to let the water run."

"I remember that," I said, "at my prima's. Marta's. The water was oily and cloudy and it had bubbles in it, but her mother, she was from México and she didn't speak English and so they didn't call."

"We called," Bobby said. "Lots of times. They did nothing."

"So why did you drink it?" Jack asked. "Or why didn't you move?"

I knew, from the look on Bobby's face, what he was thinking: Jack is this white guy who thinks you can control everything, but that's because Jack is from a family where there is money. There are people like this in México, too, of course, maybe even worse in their feeling that son mejores, above the rest of us.

"We didn't drink it out of the tap," Bobby said. "We drank soda and milk or whatever. Beer. But the thing is, you don't have to drink it. It enters through your skin when you bathe. You breathe it in the steam."

"This is what happened to Marta, too," I said, because maybe Bobby felt like Jack was calling his family stupid, as if it was their own fault they lived in a place where the water was bad. "When her family moved to este lado, they lived on that side of town. One day, she woke up, and she didn't make any sense. She tried to go to work at two in the morning and when her children talked to her, to ask her why, it was as if she were talking in a dream and so they took her to the hospital and they said—¿que dijeron?—they said there was something, *calcium?* in her blood, so much it was making her crazy."

I looked at Bobby. Was this possible? It seemed like I remembered wrong, but so many things about those days are lost to me because I loved her.

But he said, "Yes, that's what happens with lymphoma."

"And they had to put her into a coma. And then when they tried to let her wake up, she would tear the tubes out of her arms. She would say, *home*, and they would give her more shots. So she never woke up."

I looked at la niña. Estaba durmiendo. I hoped she was asleep. And I wondered, why had I told this story? Bobby didn't need to hear it. Coming from the Southside, he had heard all these stories and more and worse. And I knew, too, that one day, maybe soon, Jillian would not be sleeping. One day, she would be sitting with Angie next to the bed of her father. And I wondered, why are there places on this earth where there is more sadness than others?

6

Jillian liked the way her father smelled. When she sat next to him on the couch, she fell right back to sleep even though, in her bed, she had felt a kind of terror of falling through darkness and so she had opened her eyes to stop it, but it hadn't worked. Her heart had been beating until she thought it would jump out of her throat, but sitting next to him, and feeling his arm against her cheek and smelling him, the feeling of falling went away, became floating, and in that floating she could hear and see everything. She could see Marisol and Marta as girls playing in a creek on their nana's ranchito, she could see the way their tata put big boulders in the creek so that it would pool, and they could swim. The ranchito was down in a canyon and up above, on the rim, there were men riding horses. She could hear the sound of the horseshoes clattering on stone and there was sharp sunlight in a flat blue sky and passing clouds. She could see Marisol and Marta when they had little babies on their laps and when they were lighting candles on birthday cakes and making Halloween costumes and first Holy Communion dresses, all those things comadres do together, and then she could see Marta on the bed in the hospital room, the babies now grown into young women who would wash her and dress her after she died. Her father had done this, too, she could see. He had helped people with small things, like hanging doors for them or fixing their roofs or giving them money, and with bigger things like listening to their stories and sitting with them when they were lonely and talking to them when they were dying.

And this, Jillian knew, was the reason for falling through darkness. She knew no matter how kind her father had been, it wouldn't save him. One day, soon, within weeks, he would be walking his two miles a day and asking for tacos for dinner and the next day, it would be as if he had stepped off a cliff. His decline would be that sudden and that precipitous. For three days, Jillian knew, he would be dying and then he would die, and she wondered if she should tell him, but then she felt him put his arm behind her so she could stand up from the couch, he guided her by her shoulders, one warm hand on each shoulder to her room. She opened her eyes and sat on her bed and when she looked at his face, she knew he already knew.

Maybe he had told her, maybe that's where these voices, this knowing, came from. She wondered. He had a nana who knew things, Jillian remembered, a nana she had never met or seen but somehow, now, on this night, she could see her face and her dark hair in a braid wrapped in a circle on top of her head, she could see her hands, the long, strong fingers unpinning the circle, pulling themselves through the braids, brushing her hair at night as she sat before a mirror. Sometimes the knowing scared this nana just like it scared Jillian, but nothing seemed to scare her father.

She lay down on the bed and her dad sat next to her and he put his hand on her forehead, like when she was little, and she felt a warmth all around her heart and she knew when he was gone, this was how he would come to her, a feeling of warmth around her heart. It would always ease the fear of falling through darkness. She closed her eyes and he kissed her on the forehead, and she thought, I promise. I promise I will not let what happened to Marta happen to you. I will not let them keep you hooked up to machines in a hospital.

And he said, "I know, Mi'ja. I know you love me."

7

Angie had tried, when Bobby came back, to fast-track her forgiveness for she knew, acutely, that they had only the moment—the past had receded far away, so far as to be almost insignificant, and the future was not even a speck on the horizon. If they didn't live in the moment, they would not have a life together at all.

Of course, this is always true, she knew, you always have only the moment: just think about Glenda. Still, even with this knowledge, instantaneous forgiving was easier said than done and sometimes, when Bobby was making love to her, she couldn't help but bite him. Just a nip, really, usually on his lip or his shoulder but it would remind him to treat her very gingerly, knowing as he did, that old arguments had just intruded, his refusal to quit drinking, say, or to see a counselor.

Why had he chosen to drink, he wondered in those moments. Why had he thought coming and going with his friends was a kind of freedom? Maybe he had been too reckless, maybe she had been too rigid. Maybe. All those maybes. Maybe they had both been too young. Maybe they had both believed they could change each other, which, of course, never works. And then they had both seen other people: when she was free, he wasn't; when he was free, she wasn't. There was that white guy who earned so much more money than he did, which complicated everything in his stupid head. But why had he cared? He'd wanted to come back, it was his pride that kept him away, and he'd stayed away until it was too late to think about pride or about anything but what the heart wanted.

This grieved him, that he had made her feel less, as if drinking were more important, as if life with her was somehow not enough, as if his pride was more important. If there were only one thing he could take back, it would be this pain he had caused her. And Jillian. He had not been a good father to Jillian. He had not valued his treasures when he'd had the chance.

On those nights, as they were lying in bed, her head on his shoulder, he would distract her by talking about the house they would build someday, how they would plant mesquite trees in the backyard and hang from their branches clay pots filled with water so that the water would stay cool even in summer. He described his nana's garden, the hollyhocks, the corn and squash, chard and tomatoes, how he and his brothers had run along the rows, chasing one another in and out of the corn and in and out of the sheets hanging on the line. His nana had made tortillas, he said, under a ramada, outside under those trees, always a pot of beans simmering there next to the cast iron placa.

He loved this one song about a saint behind a glass and the smell of coffee in the mornings and he used to sing it for her, his breath ruffling her hair as they were lying there, and even though he was always off-key and had forgotten most of the words and had to hum instead, she found herself feeling calm. She didn't know why she loved hearing about his childhood so much. She could imagine the trees, their velvety green leaves, and the mourning doves, and the light from the sun. She would lie on her side, her hand on his heart and it felt, if she closed her eyes and breathed deeply, as if they had never been apart and never would be. She could see him running there, in his nana's garden, a small brown boy like the son they'd never had, his whole life in front of him.

But the truth was that most of his life was behind him and, in her opinion, much of it wasted. He never got to see the things he wanted to see, like Jerusalem or Rome or Machu Pichu. He wanted, she realized, to go to places where several layers of history were visible at once. She didn't know why this made her so sad, that he'd spent his life driving nails into two by fours and walking along the roof trestles of other people's houses, that his own life had stayed small. He hadn't even known his own daughter and would never know her now, not really, nor live to see her children.

Thinking about those things, of course, did not count as living in the moment. He still lived in the moment, even as he was dying. He always had. He had always been fully present. When you were talking to him, he listened as if you were the only person in the world. He even listened intently to Glenda's word salads, for instance, and could interpret them—when she'd lost her Alaska, he said, she wanted more ice in her water. He enjoyed each moment, making love, eating a steak, laughing at a joke, watching Jillian draw. It was as if, for him, each moment could expand infinitely, hold everything, was all that ever mattered. And more and more she did feel as if each moment contained all time, which meant it also contained the past they had already squandered and the future they would not have.

Or maybe it was simply as if time were accelerating. At night, when he was lying on the bed, watching her brush her hair, she could see him in the mirror behind her and she would suddenly feel young and desirable, beautiful simply because she was still full of life and he was looking at her. But looking at him watching her, she realized he was aging much faster than she was. He was waning. His beard was speckled with gray and the hair on his chest had strands of gray and his skin was getting dry and papery. One night, when he made love to her, she could feel his arms were not as firm as they had been even the day before. Each day he seemed to age by years. His stories, at night, were often the same stories only more and more they were peppered with the ghosts of the dead who, it seemed to her, were as present to him as she or Jillian were. He tired easily. He would fall asleep while sitting up in a chair. He was falling out of time.

One night, his arms shook as he tried to hold his weight above her and she felt his biceps with her hands. They felt like an old man's. Tears started seeping from the corners of her eyes, she couldn't help it, and he could tell, and that was the last time they ever made love.

One day, she stood next to him and said, maybe we could just lie on the bed next to each other naked and hold each other and I could put lotion on your body. Your skin is so dry.

And he had said, "Oh, Angie."

He kissed her forehead, patted her on the shoulder.

This was next to the dresser, in passing.

One day she said, "I feel as if there is a great distance between us."

One day, he said, "I am losing my words."

He said, "I am so cold."

He said, "I can't feel my legs."

And then he was gone.

And, although she and Jillian had sat by his bedside and held his hands and witnessed his last breaths, she couldn't figure it out, death. It was such a strange thing. Where had he gone? And why was everything else still the same?

8

Before he died, Jillian's father took her out to the Boneyard. He did this, she knew, because he loved planes and in the Boneyard at the Air Force base, there were thousands of them, row upon row, their sleek or fat bodies, their wings stretched out behind them, some of them with eyes and mouths painted on. Some with teeth, some with flames. They had names like Quail and Grasshopper, Skydancer and Starship. Some were named after Indians, which she thought ironic—Seminole, Iroquois, Sioux—because had anyone bothered to ask the Indians if that was okay? Then Voodoo, Banshee, Demon, their magic built in, and the Phantom II. The Phantom II was his favorite, she could tell, its sleek, supersonic lines. It had won records for time-to-climb and altitude, he told her, 98,556 feet up! And it was faster than twice the speed of sound! That's 1,485 miles per hour! he'd said. Can you imagine?

And she knew *he* could imagine. He could imagine zipping himself up in the pilot's white suit, putting the helmet on his head, slipping on the gloves, his hands on the controls. Even the little numbers and dials on the control panel he would find seductive, and the feeling of being thrust through space and time until they were one, until he had entered a dimension of pure movement, movement so fast you couldn't feel it and, of course, he equated movement with freedom. Oh, he yearned for it. He wanted to defy gravity, to go out into space, an astronaut suspended above the dear blue sphere of home.

Why leave the earth, she wondered. Why?

Because, her father said, as if he could hear her: as beautiful as it is, the earth is heavy with suffering and sorrow.

He loved the planes, it is true, especially their technological beauty, but their use grieved him. He was an ardent student of history and, therefore of warfare, and so he also pointed out the boringly named C-123s, which had dropped Agents Orange, Blue, Purple, Pink, Green, and White upon Vietnam, Laos, and parts of Cambodia—Cambodia, illegally, he said, as he was always a stickler for detail—during the Vietnam War in order to both defoliate the jungle and so deprive the enemy of cover, and to destroy crops, to deprive them of food, a lesser known objective, he said, and a possible violation of the Geneva Convention. They had dropped a rainbow of herbicides and defoliates and other dioxins, he went on, twenty million gallons, a conservative estimate, in Operation Ranch Hand.

"Operation Ranch Hand," he sighed, "how Orwellian is that? In fact, get this: the Air Force had a Smoky the Bear poster that said *Only You Can Prevent Forests!*"

Only You Can Prevent Forests!

Standing there, looking at the C-123s through a chain link fence with posted warnings about clearance and contamination, Jillian could feel the dark pools of TCE below her and she could suddenly see the planes in the air from the ground, as if she were in the jungle, the lumbering C-123s above her, five abreast, flying low to spray the herbicides, fighters flanking them in case of enemy fire. This was like a vision or a dream or a lost memory. The planes, like huge prehistoric birds, came early in the mornings, before the winds picked up. The mangroves lost their leaves right away and died, but the planes would come more than once, sometimes four or five times, because in the jungle it would take a few weeks for the other trees to lose their leaves and then they would be bare until the next rainy season. Often, they died. The crops died. The people moved from hamlet to hamlet. Again, as if in a dream, she saw a thin man, a Vietnamese man with blackened teeth, hammering together small wooden coffins. The planes come, he said, and then the babies are born without hands or limbs or something is wrong with their mouths and they can't suck and so the ones who are alive die.

Maybe, she began to think, standing next to her father, the herbicides were like the solvents, one coming from above, the other from below, but both acting as accelerants, dousing whatever was already wrong in the cells as with gasoline so that the cancers would grow like wildfire. Maybe, she thought, she was seeing into his mind, seeing his memories of movies or the news or stories he had heard. Or maybe knowledge was genetic, although, this she doubted because how different would the world be if that were true?

A year or so later, after her father died, when she was old enough to drive herself out to the Boneyard, Jillian would sit and draw pictures of the planes, of the planes still and shining, of the planes cutting through the fabric of the sky, of the people caught in and below them, of the bones left behind. It was fitting that it was called a Boneyard, she thought, the planes baking in the sun like bones in the desert, planes that had sprayed clouds of rainbow herbicides, planes that had strafed tree lines, planes that had since been washed clean with solvents, the solvents seeping into the earth, into water. The planes had been washed clean, as if they could be absolved of their role in history—which also, if she thought about it, by extension, meant the humans who had designed and flown and ordered them flown wanted also to be absolved. For why else make this monument to them? These planes had turned people to bones and the bones were lying everywhere, silenced, but bones could sing, she knew, and if she drew them in pictures, she would give them back their voices.

Lost in the Thorny Desert

*In which Jillian shares an orange with a Guatemalan man, is led
by spirits to a Borderlands dinner party, and gives birth to twins.*

1

The Babies are floating, each in his own amniotic sac, although the
cords going from what will be their belly buttons are connected to
only one placenta. The Babies, like all babies in utero, can hear mostly
vowels and not the percussion of consonants, so they hear a deep
ah-ah ee-ee-um ah-i ah-oh when the man outside is talking. If The
Babies could understand what he was saying, if they could hear actual
words, they would know this means that they are at "medium" risk,
not high but not low. They do hear the thu-thump thu-thump of their
mother's steady heartbeat, the whoosh whoosh whoosh of her blood
through arteries, and the in and out of her breath, sometimes fast, but
mostly slow. Later, they will hear echoes of these sounds in the wind
and the sea, but for now they listen to the lapping of the thick fluid
that surrounds them. They see the shadows of their mother's hands as
she strokes her belly, reassuring them with touch since she knows that
only the mother's voice goes straight into the womb and she, herself,
cannot sing to them. Beyond the dark round horizon between them
and the world, they sometimes see something bright and shining.
Maybe it is a spirit or the sun or a particularly large light bulb. This

puzzles them. Sometimes they study one another's faces or hold up a hand in greeting. Sometimes they can hear one another's thoughts, but it's hard to sustain a conversation, what with all those gurgles in their mother's digestive tract. Nice to know they are not alone, though, and, they suspect they will never feel alone, not even when they leave the universe of their mother's belly.

2

When Angie O'Malley sees her daughter's pregnant body, she can't help but think of an Aztec fertility goddess although, truth be told, she has never seen one. It's just that Jillian's belly is so round and hard and all the tattoos that she planted when she was a teenager have blossomed. Plus, Jillian's dark hair falls in waves over her very full breasts to her waist. Jillian, pregnant, may have been what Frida Kahlo was trying to dream into existence.

But why, Angie wonders, does Jillian persist with her volunteer work at this late stage? Month seven? If she were volunteering with the Food Bank, okay, but no, she is walking through the hot and thorny desert, leaving plastic bottles of water and emergency medical kits for migrants trying to make their way. Angie gets the impulse. Of course. But, shit, Jillian ought to let someone else be the Good Samaritan for once. Angie had even pointed it out to her: all her efforts could be for naught because those damn militia guys, not to mention some mean-ass Border Patrol agents, had been caught on video pouring salt into the water jugs or slashing them so that the water would seep out into the thirsty dirt.

In fact, Good Samaritans had been arrested recently and charged with felonies for taking three migrants to a hospital for care. Fifteen years! Angie told Jillian. They're facing fifteen years in prison each! What is going to happen to those babies if you get thrown in prison? Or if one of those crazy militia guys decides to take a potshot at you?

Of course, Jillian, as always, does exactly as she pleases—just like her father did. When the Samaritans pull up out front, she kisses Angie and then picks up her backpack and her white cowboy hat. I love you, she signs, on her way out the door. One of the few signs she ever bothered to learn. "I love" and then she rubs both hands over her belly. "I love" she crosses her arms across her chest and gives herself a hug, a gesture from her childhood she knows will melt her mother and all her protestations.

3

Even though she sometimes wanders off on her own, which is strictly forbidden, of course, the Good Samaritans need people like Jillian, who seem to have some kind of second sense that helps them find where the wounded or the nearly-dying-from-thirst might be hiding. They want to find them and provide them with water before they become "human remains"—way before that, way before their muscles start cramping from heat stroke and dehydration, before the nausea, before the dizziness and delirium, before…and, here, Jillian always stops herself from thinking for no one likes to think about what happens to the human body in such heat.

There are places to hide, she knows, especially when a person is afraid of coyotes, both human and animal. This desert is not barren. It can be as beautiful as it is dangerous. There is the occasional mesquite tree, its leaves velvety green in spring; only a mesquite might provide enough shade. There are fields of ocotillo, their skinny fingers orange tipped and reaching to the sky, thickets of cholla whose thorny joints will fish-hook in the skin, the ubiquitous acacia, the spiked pads of the prickly pear, and the tall dry grasses rustling. There are, Jillian has been told, over 2,000 miles of unmapped trails and that's just in the tiny area the Samaritans call the tip of the pinky finger, trails that have been used, probably, for thousands of years and that wind down into and through steep, rocky canyons. There are giant boulders in whose shade a snake might sleep, and arroyos filled with sand but that rage like rivers after the monsoons.

And then the sun. The sun, in summer, is so bright. Relentless. It bleaches the sky of color, it bakes the skin, makes heat radiate from the ground as if from an open oven. It is a dry heat that sears the nasal passages and parches the mouth, dries even the tissues of the throat and lungs. And most of the time, there is no water. As quickly as it falls from the sky, it evaporates or seeps through sand to ancient aquifers. Even someone who has a gift for hearing water will hear only the faintest of whispers far, far below. There are reasons the snakes hunt at night. Reasons this land was not inhabited, not even by those, like the Apache, whose warriors, they say, could run through the desert all day without carrying water. Maybe they carried a miracle stone in their mouths, Jillian had always thought, and from it sprang trickles of cool water.

Jillian knows she makes the Samaritans nervous, and she hates to do that to them, especially her friend who has taught her to dance, but she needs silence if she's going to hear lost or escaping souls. On this day, a cool day in early November, while the other Samaritans are leaving bottles of water and flats of cans of beans, she finds a man squatting in a tiny circle of shade. He is a small man—when he stands as if to run, she sees how small—his clothes are torn, his shoes, they have been taped together.

She holds her hand up, wait, and then puts the palms of her hands together as if to pray. Really, she thinks, she must seem strange to him, this very tall, very pregnant woman wearing a cowboy hat, appearing from nowhere, especially since she is saying nothing. She must look like an apparition, but surely she does not look dangerous. She takes off her backpack. Offers him a jug of water and the sandwich she had packed for her own lunch. They share an orange because maybe his blood sugar—and maybe hers, too, now that she thinks of it—might be low.

His skin is much darker than hers and when he speaks it is a language that is not Spanish or English. She shakes her head and shrugs, holding her hands out to indicate she doesn't understand. Then he says, "Guatemala." She nods. He gives her a piece of paper with an address in Salt Lake City. "¿Donde?" he asks. Where? So he does know at least a little Spanish.

She holds her hand up again, wait, to indicate that he should watch. She draws a line in the dirt with a stick. "¿La linea?" he asks. The border? She nods. She points with her stick in the dirt. "¿México?" She nods and then walks about six paces in the direction from which he has come and makes another line and an X and points at him. "¿Guatemala?" She nods. Then she walks back to the Mexican border and makes another X just above it and looks pointedly at him. "¿Aqui?" She nods. Yes, this is where we are. She takes two more large paces to the north and makes another X. She points at the paper with the address. "¿Utah?" She nods again.

He is about three-quarters of the way there, she guesses. One long quarter to go. He retreats back into his puddle of shade and crouches on his haunches again. She can see his face has fallen. He takes another sip of water, but a very small one. She gives him his piece of paper. If she could speak, she would say, It is still so far, yo sé, muy lejos. Lo siento. Lo siento mucho. But she isn't sure he would understand or that it would help. Her heart feels as if it is resting right on top of the shelf the babies make.

By then, two of the Samaritans have found them. They put extra tape on his shoes and give him two pairs of fresh cotton socks—because the feet are so important—and a sweatshirt because it is starting to get cold at night. They give him a bag with food and a medical kit and more water. One of them gives him some cash. Jillian eats the second sandwich she had packed for herself, feeling with each bite, piggish, although she is suddenly ravenous. The babies, she thinks, must be hungry. She watches as the Samaritans try to explain to him how to get to Tucson, where the Border Patrol stop on the highway is and how to avoid it. "Maybe hop a train in Tucson," they say, but even though they are speaking in Spanish, the man seems to understand very little.

Plus, Jillian sees, he is dazed. He is so alone. She knows, in the same way she knows how to find people—it comes to her maybe in the memories that are escaping them as they begin to let go of this life—she knows he has not always been on this journey alone, many of them started together, but then, suddenly, men with guns. Long guns. Masks. Maybe los zetas. Who can tell? Maybe the Mexican police. Somehow, for some reason, he is not in the group when the men come, he is off in the trees, maybe taking a piss, and so he sees everything through green and as if from a distance. He wants to cry out, to run towards his friends to help them, to stop the men from tying their hands behind their backs, from loading them into the beds of trucks, but he must be very quiet. Even his memory is like a nightmare that awakens him, his heart pounding, then that momentary disorientation when the fabric between sleep and waking, this world and that, is tissue thin. And yet here he is, in this even newer world, still disoriented. He feels at once grateful he escaped—his head is still on his body, after all—but guilty, guilty to have left them behind. He has been so alone since then, so alone in his grief, so weary, for even when he joined small groups of other travelers, even when they were kind and shared what little they had, they did not speak his language. Like with these large white people, their mouths moved until here and there a word would come into focus. La migra. El tren. La bestia. Riding on top of la bestia at night. The woman who fell off and lost her leg. Another thing he does not want to remember.

Jillian takes out her small notebook and tries to draw a future for him, a way to the people in Utah who are waiting. She draws their faces, their welcoming arms. She draws tamales and tortillas. Water. She draws plenty of water. Roads for him to avoid and smaller roads to follow. A train. Yes, a train might be good. A kind person in a car once he is well past the Border Patrol point, she draws that, too. Finally, maybe most importantly—how could she have forgotten?—a tiny angel up in the corner to watch over him. Before they leave him, she folds up her map and tucks it into his hand. At this point, the point of leave-taking, she feels the sadness wash over her. This? This is all the help they are allowed to give? What about loving the stranger as you love yourself? But, yes, by law, she knows this is all they can do, and staying with him or walking with him might only draw attention. She puts her hand over her heart in parting. She gives him another orange.

4

Most of the time, Baby B likes to remember his tata from the before-time, before they were in this dark warm place. He remembers how he told them to eat cake every chance they got.

Especially ice cream cake, Baby A reminds him.

Oreo cookie, in particular, Baby B thinks.

They are sure they will like ice cream cake. But then Baby B gets a little sad. Those memories of Tata in the before-time? They are already starting to fade.

Oh, I know, Baby A sighs. What did he say about the Common Good, do you remember?

That it was eroding, B says.

That's right! Baby A remembers now. Can you remember, he asks B, a time even before the before-time, when there was an overwhelming feeling of well-being? Of being one with everything?

There is no answer. He can feel that B is no longer paying attention. Instead he is practicing his transverse moves. And they have so little space now! Baby A gives him a swift kick. No response. Baby B is simply bigger and if he wants to take up more space, he will.

Must be human nature, Baby A thinks. And then he wonders: how did people ever come up with ideas they could use to justify anything and everything? Human nature? An anthropomorphic god? Couldn't they have foreseen that such a god, a god man created in his own image, that reflected his own needs and beliefs, would be dangerous? After all, such a god lets you think Manifest Destiny is a good idea. Or Dominion.

5

Jillian is looking at her cell phone. She is lost in the thorny desert, separated from the Samaritans, who had given her the phone so that the man with the fancy GPS could find her if they needed to. The face of the phone is a map. She taps it and it doesn't become a phone. It's still a map. A tiny panic starts to rise in her throat. Where the fuck are the numbers? The clock? From the sun, she knows it's past noon. How long has she been separated from the others? The panic starts to pulse. She decides to sit and listen. To eat an orange. Maybe her blood sugar is low, and this is why she can't think. Maybe, if she's quiet and still, her father's thoughts will come to her, like they sometimes did when he was living and sometimes still do when she needs him.

The orange helps. A piece of cheese helps. A few almonds and a sip of precious water. The phone is still a map, but now she knows she needs to climb up the side of the canyon even though the rocks are sharp and the way precipitous. On the ridge, her phone might become a phone again. She remembers the GPS man telling her that the reception is spotty, another reason, he had implored her not to wander. So she has to climb. But first she has to pee. One of the babies is resting right on her bladder. She should pee down here, not up on the ridge, although, she's sure if she pulled down her pants on the ridge, someone would spot the white moon of her butt. That will be the solution of last resort, she tells herself, she will drop her drawers.

Climbing up—such slow going, what with the loose rocks and the big boulders. She has to stop every few feet to catch her breath. How, she wonders, do those migrant women keep up when they're pregnant? And if they don't keep up? Well, they're strong, she thinks, as strong as she is, but they're still often left behind. And they often don't have the right shoes. She, at least, has good hiking boots. And she knows the Samaritans won't leave her behind, but they have to find her before they can take her with them. That's her job. To make sure they find her.

When she stops to catch her breath, she stands very still and listens, not this time for the escaping memories of the dying but for the calls of the living. Plus, her white hat might reflect the sun. Plus, she tries to use the face of her phone, which is still a map, as a mirror, to signal SOS, SOS: vessel, carrying two babies, in distress! She's watched enough reruns of *MacGyver* to know it's the small things that can save you.

Once she's up on the ridge, she stands very still and puts her hands on the babies. It's okay, she thinks to them, rubbing her hands around in two overlapping circles, it's okay. She feels a spasm. Weird. She hasn't felt that before. The panic starts to rise again, but then she sees they are surrounded by ghosts and although she finds ghosts, or spirits, in general, reassuring, there are so many of them, so many that have perished that she is worried they have come to help her cross over.

No, she tells herself. No. Not yet. They are here to guide you to the living. It is going to be okay, she thinks to her babies. I promise. Your tata will help us.

They're not moving much, the babies, but her body's motion, the climbing, has probably lulled them to sleep. She should be hungry, but instead she's a little nauseous. She drinks some water for good measure. Thinks about her last orange but decides to save it. Puts a hard candy in her mouth instead and pretends it's a stone, a smooth stone, like the ones she imagined the Apache warriors always held in their mouths, a small eternal spring of water.

She looks at the phone. Still a map. Her thumbprint doesn't work. There are no numbers. Siri doesn't answer. What the fuck?

Breathe. Now let go of it—it's her father's voice she hears now, she's sure. She can hear him as clearly as if he were on the phone. He says: you are on the ridge. Good job. This is the best place for you to be, Jillian. You can see for miles. You don't have to hide. If someone sees you, that's a good thing. The sun is behind you, so that's the west. I know logic tells you to walk west, Mi'ja, but walk to the east. Trust me. Be careful. It's still warm enough for snakes. Remember everything you know about the desert. You still have water. You still have food. Your legs and your mind are strong. Just listen. Listen for signs. The wind is coming towards you. It's carrying voices. Do you hear them? There is a dinner party. Music. Maria-chis. Laughter. Listen.

And she does hear them. The violins first, then human voices, the clinking of silverware against dishes. She sees the wall, now, like a crooked line. The color of dried blood, it has spaces between the tall slats and, along the top, a broad band. You couldn't squeeze through the slats, you couldn't climb over without ladders, but you could reach your hand between the rusted slats, and touch someone, the hand of your grandmother, maybe, or the soft hair on a baby's head. Or, if you were someone, like that Border Patrol guy, you could reach your hand through with your gun and shoot someone, like that teenaged boy, in the back, as he was running towards home on the other side. How many bullets? Jillian tries to remember, the anger rising. How many bullets in his back?

Don't, her father tells her. Don't, the chorus of the dead tells her, don't think about that now. One of them might find you. One of them might help. Think about that. Think about the babies. Call them to you, if you can.

She stops for a minute, out of breath again, although she is not climbing. The babies are still in the cradle of her body. She strokes them with her hands, but they give no sign that they feel her. She feels another spasm, a pressure that begins in the middle of her back and moves forward, around her. She can feel her belly getting hard as it moves. It's too early, she thinks, they must be Braxton Hicks, her body getting ready. Normal for the thirty-fourth week. Normal. This is normal. Or it might be dehydration, simple dehydration, so she stops and drinks a few more sips of water. She eats the last orange.

Oh, Babies, she rubs her belly, how she loves them. Already. And she doesn't even know them. She wonders if they can hear the music, too. Do the spirits hear it? They must for they are streaming towards it in almost giddy anticipation. She starts to walk towards the sound again. The music has stopped but the wind is carrying all of the voices. And then she sees it, the long dining table that dissects the wall, one half on this side of the border and one half on el otro lado. There is a tablecloth and, on the cloth, painted, a woman's eyes, one eye on each side of the border, as if she is looking to the heavens. There is a mariachi band, one half on one side of the border, the other half on the other. The woman's eyes shift from the heavens and gaze directly at Jillian and the spirits on the ridge as if to say, Come, come and join us. The people who are seated around the table, stand or turn and stand. They all look in her direction.

She waves her cowboy hat at them, but isn't sure they see her. Maybe they are looking at something else and, when she turns to look behind her, she sees a halo around the sun. In the halo, on either side of the sun, a smaller sun. A dogsun. It's a good sign, she thinks. Even the people are pointing at it. She wonders if that's what they're celebrating, some kind of celestial event. Día de los Muertos was last weekend, she knows, the dead were honored then, reunited with their living in graveyards all over Mexico, so maybe this dinner party is for those who have no graves, for those whose families are still searching.

No wonder the spirits are whispering. No wonder they feel festive. The mariachis start playing again, the people are again talking to one another and passing serving plates, and Jillian continues to follow the spirits along the ridge. When it's time to climb down, her father reminds her, Lean back into the ridge so, if you fall, you won't go head over heels. So you'll slide on your butt.

So I won't land on the babies, she thinks, but if she descends now, she won't be able to see the dining party. She needs the elevation to know where to go, but she wants to navigate that side of the ridge before the sun goes down. The desert, at night, is like the sea. It can swallow you.

6

"¡Juana! ¡La virgen! ¡Mira, la virgen! And she's waving a cowboy hat! And she is great with child!" It was Nardo who first saw her. We didn't know it was Jillian, pues, and so of course, we all laughed. We thought it was the sun in his eyes. The sun was very strange that day. Or maybe we thought it was la cerveza. Nardo es muy chistoso, siempre, but especially after a few beers.

Still he insisted. He was going to go and climb that cliff to help la virgen, pero, tu sabes, we were on this side and she was on that, so no era possible. That Nardo, he still thinks that he is joven y muy fuerte, but we all know how that goes. He called to his sobrinos at the other end of the table, en el norte, because they are much younger and stronger than he is, but it took a while for them to believe him. ¿La Virgen? ¿Embarazada? ¿Aqui?

¡Oh, pobrecita Jillian! By the time they got to her, she was muy, muy cansada. She could barely walk. Her legs were shaking. I am sure her angels must have guided her. In fact, I could feel them when they brought her to me, I could feel them still around her. Y Victor y Enrique, ellos me dijeron que, when they found her, she touched their hands as if to test that they were real. She had come so far, how far, we didn't know. How long had she been wandering? ¿Quien sabe? No one knows porque ella no puede hablar, ni en ingles, ni en español. But it couldn't have been longer than a day, especially not in her condition porque, es la verdad, she was very large with child. When they found her, she was sitting on a boulder. She had come almost all the way down from the ridge by herself and she had fallen at least once, es cierto, because her hands were cut up and the knees of her jeans, torn, and the butt of her pants dirty, as if she'd slid in the dirt. She had, beside her, a pack with an almost empty bottle of water, some hard candy, and a cell phone—eso era todo, no había comida, ni más agua—so, if we hadn't found her, one day in the desert, sin agua, and not to mention los animales...cougars. Coyotes. I don't want to think about what would have happened.

She was drawing in a small notebook when they found her sitting there. She was drawing the dinner party, even the eyes on the table-cloth and the strange sun above. There was a pregnant woman—herself, ¿entiendes?—and she was surrounded by wisps of figures, one with the face of her father. And she had drawn two men. Victor and Enrique? And on the drawing, one name—here, I can show it to you—one name, ¡Juana de Dios! Y es muy extraño porque we were not going to go to that party porque Junie was not feeling well y tu sabes, I hate to leave him alone, but at the last minute, Nardo wrapped him up in a blanket and put him in his little doggy bed at my feet in the truck. Nos vamos, Nardo me dijo, and so we went! When Victor first spoke to her, she showed him the drawing and pointed to the table, y me dijo que, when he saw my name, he felt the hair rise on the back of his neck, he felt the cold air of the ghosts around her. He was glad she had already touched him because that's how he knew *she* was not a ghost. She tried to stand up on her own, but she was so weak, they had to get one on each side of her to help her walk. By the end, they almost had to carry her.

Nardo, he is my viejito and I love him, but she is a tall girl. Very tall. And with that baby? Y tú sabes que, at the time, we thought it was only one baby, solamente uno. Nunca did we think there might be two. Nunca, con su corazón, could Nardo have carried her. Mi amor, I told him, it is enough that you saw her! Otherwise, el desierto would have taken three more. Tres. Y so close to those who could help them. Ay, dios mío, what would I have told her mother?

7

Baby A has been head-down for a few weeks, barely moving except to jab his mother with an occasional jazz hand or to nudge his brother with an elbow or a foot in a bid for more room. He has been focused and intense, conserving his energy for the main event. *It* is going to happen soon, he thinks to his brother. I don't know what *it* is, exactly, but I feel *it* is coming.

Could you be any more vague?

Can't you feel the change? The pressure? We are going to have to leave this place. I think that's what *it* is. A parting. A letting go. A something new.

Baby B sighs. He is content to stay in the dark warm place. It is safe. There is plenty of food and, so far, enough room for him to stretch and practice his somersaults. He is in no hurry to leave. And he has company, his brother, whom he can ignore if he so chooses. Which he does, right now, he wishes to ignore him. Blah blah blah. That's his brother, always worrying.

Don't you remember, in the before-time, how Tata told us about the thing called birth. I think that's what *it* is. We might be pushed through a dark tunnel, he said, but then we would come into this big place with light. It would be cold at first, but she would be waiting for us. She would hold us against her heart and keep us warm and she would still feed us with her body. Remember?

B pauses, mid-somersault. It is hard for him to imagine anything better than this place, this feeling of being surrounded by warmth, of always being satiated, this swimming, this sleeping, this dreaming.

But think of all those things Tata told us about! Baby A continues. Ice cream cake. Wind. Sunshine. There is a thing called running through the grass. Flying a kite. You would have all the space you want and then, when you want it, she will hold you in her arms, she will be soft, she will still rock you and feed you and protect you, although in different ways.

Baby A is trying to put a positive spin on *it*, the thing called birth. He knows it is inevitable and coming soon, but even he wonders, what happens if you don't like it? If you want back inside? He knows different ways of being and a different world will be scary. What if you want to be one with her again? He is not sure you have a choice. What if something happens to her? *What if something happens to her*?! Was that a possibility? Had Tata ever said?

¡Ya bastante! Baby B moves as high up as he can, away from his brother and just under her ribs. He wants to feel her heartbeat

and her lungs massaging his back. He wants the whoosh whoosh whoosh of his mother's arteries to drown out his brother's thoughts and anxieties. Why would she ever make them leave?

8

Jillian remembers sitting on the boulder, feeling its warm roundness beneath her, knowing she has gone as far as she can by herself—oh, she knows she is not alone, the others, the spirits, they still surround her, they will never leave her, and she can hear her father's voice, still telling her, only a little farther, Mi'ja, a little farther, you have to do it, Mi'ja, you can do it. But her legs will not hold her. Her legs shake when she tries; she is afraid of falling again. What if, the next time, she lands on the babies? She has to envision the next thing, what will happen, it is her only hope. And so she sits on the warm boulder and takes one of her last sips of water and lets her hand begin to move across the page. This, she thinks, is what they mean by an act of faith.

The next thing she remembers, two men standing before her. Miss? they ask, Miss? But are they of the flesh? She is not sure. She touches their hands; her hands do not go through them. Their hands are warm. She shows them the map of her future, and so of the Babies' future. She chooses the one with the kindest face and she presses the map into his hand and, with her heart, implores him for more help than she had been able to give the Guatemalan.

The next thing she remembers? The faces of women, all around her. She is lying down on a bed. She sees in their faces that they, too, have had life grow inside them; they remember being as she is, helpless against the pain, the pain that comes in waves from the middle of the back and squeezes towards the belly button. She sees that some of them have lost their babies and that the sorrow is still alive in them. They have their hands on her to share their strength. Give in to the pain, the women tell her, give in to it. It will wash through you then, and you can relax until the next one. Respira, their hands say, breathe.

This moment is when she notices that she is holding her breath, just as she must have been holding it all day as she walked along the ridge, holding it in fear, but now she has to let go of that fear. Respira como esto, the women say, and they all take deep inhales together, just when she should, and then exhale, slowly, their lips pursed. Inhale, exhale. Inhale, exhale. And so Jillian does. Trust your body, the women say. Trust your body. Is there music? It seems like there is music. Violins. Guitars. As if through a window at night.

And then there is the voice of Juana of God! So the men had followed the map! She hears the jingling of Juana's many bracelets as she takes them off, the clink of her many rings in a bowl. Juana of God is washing her hands. Juana of God is saying, ¡Nardo! ¡Tráeme Junie! Necessito su ayuda. Jillian understands, then, that the Babies are about to be born. Even though it is early. Maybe too early. And then Juana's face. And then her voice again, softer, Mi'ja. Oh, pobrecita. Pero no te preocupes. You are safe now. The baby is fine. Everything will be all right.

Jillian holds up her hand with two fingers to tell Juana, *Two. There are two babies.* But just then, she has a feeling that is different from the others, stronger, so strong she leaves her body, floats up near the ceiling, and she sees herself on the bed. She feels like a deer, lying in the tall grass. She is hiding, waiting for her body to do the next thing. She watches as Nardo brings Junie in. She sees Junie's head wrench back as if he has been shot by arrows. She sees the spirits leave Junie and gather around Juana and then Juana, she transforms, becomes someone who knows whatever she needs to know as always happens when the spirits come into her.

Jillian sees her body on the bed, sees she is only her body, an animal body. She sees two women behind her, holding her up, and then sees two other women, on either side of her, each holding a leg. Her body tells her to push, to push as if she has to take a giant shit, to push as she has never pushed before. The breathing in, then out, the pushing with the breath. That's it, Mi'ja, the women say, listen to your body, it will tell you what to do and when. She sees Juana between her legs. Juana is whispering, sí sí sí, praying, santísima madre de Dios, pedimos su ayuda.

Jillian's body pushes again, a long hard push, and a big fish slips bloody between her thighs.

With that, her mind is back in her body, and a woman, not Juana, is holding a baby upside down by his feet. ¡Un niño! The woman says. He is a little blue. There is a pulsing cord. He cries, all on his own. Juana, still at the foot of the bed, between her legs, seems to be waiting for something. The afterbirth?

There is another contraction, a strong one, and suddenly Jillian remembers. She holds up two fingers again. Don't forget the other one, she wants to say. She starts clapping her hands. Listen! She waves her hand with two fingers. But Juana is in her trance, she cannot see or hear her cries, and most of the women are gathered around the baby already born. They think she is crying from joy.

Jillian grabs on to the arms of two women still standing on either side of her and pulls herself into a squatting position on the bed. Some say she screamed.

9

"They say she screamed," Juana told Angie. "Pero no sé. What do I know? I was not there, tú sabes. Junie sent some very strong spirits that night, maybe even la Virgen. Muy misterioso, this going out of your body and your mind, if might I say so, and then coming back in once everything is over. Pobrecito Junie. Ay, Junie. He gave his life for your Jillian."

And here Juana was overcome again. She and Angie were sitting on the porch of the women's collective, drinking coffee and eating Juana's favorite pastries. She remembered how, when she came out of her trance and saw Jillian and the two babies, she had gone over to Junie. He was lying on his side in his bed. He was panting. His eyes, those cute bug eyes, were still rolled up in his head. He did not come out of his trance when she came out of hers. Nunca had this happened before. She knew, then, that he was going to the flower world. She picked him up and held him. Oh, Junie, she'd crooned. We have to thank you for your gifts, for bringing the spirits and only the good spirits, and for your love. Never did you ask for anything in return. Oh, Junie, mi amor, gracías.

Angie grasped Juana's hand. She had already thanked her, did not know how else to thank her for the life of her daughter and the two babies. It was true that Junie had died that night, and even an ordinary dog is irreplaceable, Angie knew, to those who loved him. But Junie? Where would they ever find another Chihuahua who could channel spirits? And if Junie was dead, so was Juana's career, although she had not said as much, nor did she seem to care. At least not yet.

"Oh, Juana," Angie said, "lo siento. Lo siento mucho. I know you loved him. I know you will miss him. And I will be grateful, always."

Juana put her hand on her heart, which felt as if it might break all over again. She knew Junie had chosen to sacrifice himself just as she had known, when she told Nardo to bring him into the room, that it would probably kill him, this last channeling, he was so old, so weak. He had not been well for years, really, but what else could she do?

Juana gave a huge sigh. "It happens that sometimes an animal gives his life for a human," she told Angie, "no one knows why or how. Fue un milagro, pues. The whole night was a miracle on so many counts."

She had already told Angie about the miracle of Nardo seeing Jillian up on the ridge and insisting that his nephews go and help her. And Angie had seen the map to the dinner party that Jillian had drawn with Juana's name on it, so that was miracle number two, if anyone was counting.

"Getting Jillian over to the women's collective on this side of the border was *not* a miracle," Juana said, "because going north to south never is."

But it *was* a miracle, miracle number three, that the dinner party was that night: not only so Jillian could see it and be guided by it, but also because of the strange sun that drew their attention to her, especially Nardo's, and because it meant that so many people were there, especially women, who could help Juana, and finally, because it meant that Juana, herself, and Junie were there. Especially because, as Juana had already explained, they had not planned on coming, but Nardo had got it into his head at the last minute that they should. Something just told me, he said to Juana, over and over again, shrugging.

"Claro," Juana said to Angie, pausing to take a bite of her pastry, "I should listen to Nardo more often. But don't tell him that. He's already growing, como se dice, a big head. He's telling everyone how he saved Jillian y los niños from certain death in el desierto. And, okay, es la verdad. But he had a little help!

"So this, as I say, is what they say about that night," Juana continued. "It could have happened, pero yo no recuerdo nada. Y parece fantástico, yo sé. But the women, they say after Jillian pulled herself up and screamed, el primero answered. La mujer who was holding him by his little ankles, she swears that he said—el *bebé* dijo—¡no se olviden de mi hermano!—and then, Don't forget el segundo! as if he were translating for his mother. And so la mujer told them: ¡Ayudale a Jillian! ¡Hay otro bebé!

"Yo sé. ¡Es increíble! Pero ellas me dijeron que only then did Jillian lie back and only then, it is said, did I help her with el segundo. It could not have been easy because they say I had to reach up inside her. It was as if that baby did not want to come out and the first one, some say, he kept calling, *Brother, brother, aqui está, our mother is here, and she wants us to come out. Hermano, remember what Tata said. There will be cake! Y helado! Oreo cookie!*

"Of course, it is hard to understand what a baby says, muy difícil, even a baby much older than this one, and so there is some disagreement about what he said, exactly. And, as I'm sure you can imagine, there was quite a bit of confusion and the women, themselves, they were probably praying and calling out to the baby to encourage him to come out.

"So, at any rate, a few remember el primero talking, but most, they do not, they were so overcome con el nacimiento del segundo hijo and so busy helping. ¡Qué milagro! they kept crying. They couldn't believe it! A second baby! They say I had to reach way up and grab him by his feet, they say I had to pull and pull to get him out, pobrecito, and that is why his feet and legs are so bruised. Y Jillian, pobrecita, that is why she is so tired and so sore."

Juana paused. "Tú sabes que, en español, when you want to say, 'to give birth,' you say, 'dar a luz,' pero 'dar a luz' signifca, en ingles, 'to give light,' and she did, she gave us light twice, but it took a lot out of her."

Angie had been picking at her food. She looked at Juana and felt full of gratitude and love, for Juana and for all of those who had helped Jillian, and full of joy that both babies were alive, although they were so tiny as to seem fragile, which scared her. She was afraid to love them—who was it, in what culture, during what time period? when they didn't even give babies names until they were at least three years old? This is how she felt. Cautious. She never wanted to have her heart broken again. Bobby. Bobby had broken it enough.

She was also full of sorrow for what Jillian had gone through—oh, Jillian, when she'd seen her in the morning, she had seemed traumatized, *blank*, whether from the pain or the trek or both—she was holding the babies, yes, lying on her side, both of them swaddled next to her, sleeping, her hand softly circling and circling on their tummies as she had when they were inside her, but she? Where was she? And when would she come back into herself?

And, then she, Angie, she felt lonely, almost empty because Bobby was not there to see his nietos, the little babies he would have held so tenderly. And sad for Jillian because her father did not live to see them, their light in the world, as Juana had just said.

"Angie," Juana was saying, "Angie, mi amiga, pienso que la niña,"—
for she still thought of Jillian as a girl and would never, in all her many
years left to come, think of her otherwise—"pienso que Jillian should
stay and rest for at least a few more days, maybe a week or two. I
have been making teas for her to help her blood get strong again and
to help her milk come in. It would be good to wait until the babies
are bigger, don't you think? The road back to your home is such a
long one, especially with all the ruts from the monsoons, which, as
we know, they will never repair. Besides, todos los vecinos quieren
conocer a los bebés. They want to bring gifts, of course. They want
to know if the babies will talk again and they wonder this, have the
babies seen anyone who has just passed? Do they have messages? Or
can they see the future? Or can Jillian draw for them a map?

"It isn't so much for them to ask, really, is it, Angie? But they want
for her to rest first. Y, por supuesto, I want to invite you, if it is not
too much trouble for you and Jillian and the babies, I would want
you to help me bury my Junie."

10

Junie was buried in the garden of the women's collective where they
grew vegetables and medicinal herbs. Ashes to ashes, dust to dust.
Go back to the earth, Junie, Juana had said, nourish it, even though
you were so much of the spirit.

"After all," she said, "the line between body and soul is mutable,
a border one crosses every day and every night, a liminal space like
air over the surface of water. Somewhere, invisible to the human
eye," she said, "things that seem different are really the same, como
el aire y el agua son los mismos. There is a space, right on the surface
of a lake, where air molecules sink into the water just as the water
molecules rise to meet them. We are all, como se dice, mist, we are
all mist, niebla, fog, fantásmas. Ni aquí, ni allá, pero son los mismos,
juntos. In death, as in life, the spirit lives."

For a while after the birth, Jillian felt exactly as Juana had described it: as if she were neither here nor there, as if she were a ghost of herself, somewhere between the living breathing mother she needed to be and the girl who was wandering the desert as one with spirits. The tiny babies, of course, their bodies that needed tending, their mouths pulling on her nipples, their tiny hands reaching out to touch her breasts, their breath like mist on her neck as she burped them, they drew her back into physical life, just like, when she was giving birth to them, she'd felt she was only her animal body, her function to split, to open, to push them into Juana's hands where, if her body did die, they would still survive.

But, of course, they were also of the spirit because when she gazed into their eyes, she could see pure soul, pure light, pure love. They were, each of them, a self already, a self separate from her. They each had a name she had not yet discovered, but they were also, each of them, a line back to her father, back to her mother and her mother's mother, a tether to the past and future at once, securing her, as if with scar tissue, to this world.

And they were still keyed into her consciousness, their minds one with hers and, in this way, without speaking, the babies told her everything they knew. They told her what their tata had told them in the before-time, that a dark time was coming, darker even than when he was a child and punished for speaking Spanish on the school grounds. There was one thing called ice that was melting quickly, and another thing called ICE that was clearly evil. At the border, children would be separated from their parents and taken to places that were very cold. Sometimes they would be placed in homes, but then they would disappear from them without a trace. A new kind of desaparecidos! Baby A even spoke of visions of orphans being put in warehouses and made to make cell phones with their tiny hands. That is in a place called China, Baby B said, and you have to *dig* to get to China. But Baby A continued: plants will shrivel under the sun, the air will become particulate, rivers will sink beneath the ground or catch on fire. Ice will melt and seas will rise. Water will become more precious than oil, whatever that is. Yes, B knew all that was true, already true in many places and not only in some far-off future, but he wasn't going to encourage Baby A, who was already wound a little tight, in his opinion, a little too intense. What about the ice cream and running in the grass? B asked. Flying kites? Why don't we think about that stuff? B had been reluctant to come, yes, but now that he was here, he was going to make the best of it.

Jillian, too, knew that the babies' visions were not so far from this reality. She remembered how the Border Patrol had slashed the plastic water bottles left for those whose thirst could kill them in one day, how they had punctured the cans of beans left by the Samaritans, too. Then she remembered the two men who had come to the ridge and brought her to Juana, the women who had surrounded her bed and helped her with the births. They had very little and yet, every day, they fed her. She wondered if the babies, since they'd been born here, in Mexico, if that gave them the right to become citizens. It was something she would have to google.

And so, when Angie needed to leave, Jillian was not ready, not physically and not philosophically. She stayed, in fact, for months and during that time the vecinos came and wanted to talk to the babies. Jillian would bring them out to the courtyard in the mornings and, one by one or two by two, los vecinos would come and talk to them. ¿Entienden español? they would ask, and Jillian would shrug. She held up her finger and thumb to indicate un poquito. Very little. The babies, being pleasant babies, always smiled or sometimes fell asleep. Jillian loved it when the little old men would touch the babies' feet and say patas saladas because, although she had no idea why they said "salty feet," she remembered her tata saying that to her when she was little.

"They are just ordinary babies," Juana told the vecinos, "milagros, sí, como todos los bebés, but they do not talk. Ni en ingles, ni en español. Just like their mother. El Primero has not spoken again and, en realidad, maybe he never talked. Maybe las mujeres were hearing panic and loneliness in his cry," she said, "the panic and loneliness of being torn from his mother and of leaving his brother behind. Puede ser. They were hearing what he wanted to say and what Jillian wanted to say and so, if you think about it," she told them, "it is the women who brought about the miracle of El Segundo's birth. It is the women who were miraculous because they could hear what was needed without words.

"Es como Jillian," Juana told them, "because Jillian cannot speak, she has been given the gift of listening and this is why she can hear spirits escaping and spirits rising and why she can follow them. And, this is a gift that can be cultivated just as the plants in the garden can be cultivated. If you are very still," Juana told them, "like Jillian, you will hear whatever you need to hear from both the living and the dead, from the future and the past. You will not need the babies to tell you anything."

And so Jillian, learning from Juana and not wanting to draw the dark future the babies saw, did not draw maps that would lead people north—after all, she didn't know if the man from Guatemala had ever made it to Salt Lake City and the map she had drawn for herself, which had indeed saved her, had taken her farther to the south.

Instead of drawing maps, she drew visions of future gardens. The women's collective had already turned el desierto into an oasis that fed many families. She drew rows of plants growing, small animals, like chickens and rabbits. She drew children. She drew people gathering food that grew in the desert, mesquite pods for grinding into flour, the soft pads and fruit of the prickly pear, people making adobes from mud and allowing them to dry in the sun. She drew water, of course, being collected in cisterns, and jarras con agua hanging from trees, hollyhocks with vines climbing them, just as her father had described his nana's garden. Essentially, she drew the life she saw around her. After all, things might get worse before they got better. The area was being flooded with refugees from farther south because of the cartels and the hunger for drugs en el norte. There would be more and more mouths to feed here in the frontera and there was the drought to consider.

Once Jillian was stronger and the babies were older, she and Juana took trips into town. Sometimes Juana pointed out the bad places, like the gym built by the cartel and their big houses with the high walls, the broken glass embedded along the top.

"Parece un carcel," Juana told her, "¿no? A prison of their own making."

Sometimes Jillian waited outside on a bench while Juana went into this one particular shop. Each time Juana went in, Jillian noticed, she came out with fewer of her many rings and bracelets and then her hands, when she gestured as she talked, did not make the music they used to make.

11

On the day Angie was coming to take Jillian and the babies home, Jillian drew Juana's home, la casa blanca, in Magdalena. It was a large home, an estate, really, that was painted white, as white as San Xavier del Bac in Tucson, the white dove of the desert. Outside, San Xavier was white, but inside, alive with color, geometric patterns, flowers, babies, angels on clouds, angels carrying chains or fish, every inch covered in color, and so Jillian started drawing murals on the outside of la casa blanca, to transform it from a house of spirit to a house of the earth. Then she drew people in the lush courtyard, people like Aunt Glenda in her wheel chair, and old people, like her grandmother before she had died, old people whose minds were out-of-time. Al otro lado, as she had begun to think of the north, those people were sometimes tied in chairs in nursing homes, the chairs lined the halls and the old women cried for their mothers. But here, they would be able to roam within the walls and the courtyards of la casa blanca without worry. At the top of the drawing, Jillian wrote the words la casa de los viejitos.

When Angie arrived, Jillian showed her the drawing. Her mother had almost always—except when Jillian was a teenager, of course—been able to interpret her work accurately. "Ah," she said, "yes."

Angie showed the drawing to Juana and explained to her that there was a town in Europe—where? she could not remember, exactly—where people with dementia lived. They could wander the streets, have a coffee in a café and talk to others, they could go into a little store and buy candy, and then they went home to their rooms. The people who worked in the stores and cafés were actually their care-givers, but the viejitos didn't know that. Instead of living in the worst of all worlds when they were old, they were living in one of the best!

"This is what Jillian is telling you, Juana. Now that you don't have Junie, turn la casa blanca into a casa for los viejitos. In the US, they are cutting Medicaid. The old and the sick, when their families can't care for them, when their families don't have enough money, what will happen to them? In the end, with my mother and Glenda to take care of, even though I had Marisol to help me? Era impossible. I had to put my mother into a place where she cried all the time, they were all crying, and it was muy muy caro. They take all this money from you but they do not pay the women who take care of the old anything at all! Es loco, muy loco. Don't get me started. But. Anyways...

"What I'm saying"—Angie took both of Juana's nearly ringless hands into her own—"people will bring their parents to you, their children with brain injuries from IEDs or accidents or mass shootings or beatings by the cops or enraged lovers, all those things that happen en el norte, and they will pay you to take care of them and you will take better care of them and it will cost less than in the States. Juana, think about it! It gives you a way of healing people's lives without Junie."

"¿Casa de los viejitos?" Juana mused. "¿Por qué no? ¿Como se dice? Outsourcing?"

"Outsourcing the care of the elderly and the permanently brain-injured. Yes," Angie said. "It would be a gift."

Juana was an enterprising woman, in addition to being well-intentioned, and she could see the possibilities immediately. ¿Casa de los Desorientados? House of those who have been left behind? House of the forgotten ones—Casa de los Olvidados. That had a nice ring to it. And it was memorable. She shook her head at the irony.

"You norteamericanos," she said, "already you come to us for medicines and to see our dentists. And to Costa Rica for operations. ¿Por qúe no, pues?" She laughed. "Nardo would fit right in! Las viejitas love him."

It took a long time to say their farewells—not goodbyes, because Jillian knew she would often return to the collective and would often visit Juana to help start La Casa de los Olvidados. She would return to help because, with the babies, she would no longer be able to walk with the Samaritans.

As soon as Angie and Jillian turned on to the main road out of the collective, as soon as Juana disappeared from the rear-view mirror, Angie said to Jillian, "You know, if you don't give them names soon, Primero and Segundo are going to stick."

And, yes, Jillian knew. But the babies still had not told her their names. And wasn't that just like her mother? To be already commenting on Jillian's maternal deficiencies?

In order to redirect the conversation, Jillian pointed the wrong way to the Border Station. She wanted her mother to drive them to the park along the border on this side. There was a sidewalk and stations where you could stop and do push-ups or other exercises; there were benches and trees and tables for picnics. There were old men, sitting and talking, and mothers pushing babies in strollers. When Jillian looked through the fence, she could see barren desert on the other side, but on this side, no. They had done their best to make something beautiful. They had painted portraits of la virgen, for instance, and of a giant baby peering over to el norte.

This was near the place of the dinner party, the one that had called to Jillian, the one where the table had straddled the border and where, on the tablecloth, the woman's eyes were staring at heaven. But that was not Jillian's favorite part. No, the part of the park Jillian liked most was where the people had painted the wall blue, and so the wall, especially as you approached it from a distance, disappeared. It became a part of the desert sky behind it.

Los Niños Perdidos

In which Jillian lives with Primero and Segundo in Magdalena and helps Juana of God in La Casa de los Olvidados and, as a result, comes to know, in the Biblical sense, Charlie-Carlos.

1

Primero and Segundo are two years old before they first journey with their mother to the Casa of the Forgotten Ones. Until then, because the border has been militarized, Jillian has been going by herself so that she can paint the walls of the Casa without worrying about them following her up the scaffolding.

Primero, everyone knows, can climb like a monkey. And Segundo, his forte? He is mechanically inclined. He likes to sit in Aunt Glenda's lap in the chair with big wheels because she lets him move the lever that propels them forwards and back.

Now that Marisol has followed Bella and Stevie Jr. to college in California, it is Aunt Glenda—actually, Great-aunt Glenda—with whom the twins spend their days while their nana is at work. The boys have jobs to do. Primero must climb up on the counters to get the dishes from the cupboard, and the bread and the peanut butter, while Segundo takes the leftover already-cooked bacon out of the fridge and nukes it, just so, who toasts the bread, again just so, just so that it is warm and toothsome but not too toasty. Primero then spreads the peanut butter and Segundo lines up the bacon on top, the edges of the strips touching but not overlapping, and when Aunt Glenda says, "Oh, the moon, it was so sweet," Primero understands that she wants maple syrup or perhaps golden honey drizzled, labyrinthine, over the bacon.

Glenda, left to her own devices, would spend the whole day watching television. She cries easily, understandable since this is what she sees: children exiting schools in an orderly line, one hand on the shoulder of the one in front; yellow boats on the seas, full of children, and worse, children's bodies washed up on the shore; chain link enclosures that look like dog kennels but are, instead, full of children; caravans of refugees crossing desert lands, yes, full of children, exhausted, thirsty, hungry, tear-stained children. It all makes Glenda cry, tapping as it must into a deep river of grief. She cries until her toast is soggy, until the tears begin to pool on her tray and then drip down onto the floor. She cries until the twins are afraid they might drown in the salty sea she is creating.

At this point, unless they want to get out the mop, which they don't, the boys have to climb up on the chair with her. While Primero pats her face and smooths her hair, Segundo switches to cartoons and then hides the remote. Primero gives her his version of a kiss, lips pressed tightly together against her cheek. Segundo, too, he kisses her, but on her withered right hand. Then he presses the lever and off they go towards the front door, down the ramp, and out into the sunshine.

While they are on their walk, they often wonder why it is called a walk. Still, they enjoy the fresh air, the tall trees, the birds. "The moon, the moon!" they point at the silver sliver when it is visible in the pale sky. "Plane! Plane! Bye bye!" They wave. "Bye bye!"

And so to other walkers, to those who are watering their lawns or washing their cars, to those who don't understand Twin, they seem like ordinary two-year-olds.

But these two-year-olds cannot forget what they've already seen.

"And so it is coming to pass," Primero says to Segundo in Twin, "just as Tata in the before-time told us it would: this is what happens when the-world-as-my-oyster philosophy meets religion."

"It's called Prosperity Theology," Segundo reminds him.

"Dominion," Primero responds. "Although, as we have seen, El Chillón has no religion. He does, however, believe in Dominion."

El Chillón, the Crybaby. This is what their nana calls him. El Chillón and His Minions. But to hear Primero say it aloud makes Segundo a little nervous. He doesn't yet know that not all people understand Spanish—although he has figured out, from forays to the grocery store, that not all people like Spanish-*speakers*. So to say El Chillón in public? Either way, whether the people around them understand or not, it could be bad news. He surveys their surrounds.

"Hiya!" he says to a man in a red baseball cap.

"All morally bereft," Primero continues, as obsessed as he is oblivious. "El Chillón believes in nothing."

"*Nothing!*" Aunt Glenda shouts, as they roll along down the sidewalk, Segundo waving and smiling at all the possibly-unmedicated, possibly-armed adults they pass. "*Nothing! Zero! Zip! Zilch! Nada! Naught! Nil! Rien! Nichts! Nulla! Niente!*"

Glenda sometimes surprises the babies by understanding their conversations. Of course, the boys are nothing if not quadrilingual. They speak not only Twin, but also understand English, some Spanish, and of course, Glenda's Word-salad-ese.

"It's a good thing we're babies," Segundo says to Primero, still waving as if they're in a parade.

"A good thing we look white," Primero nods, waving to one questionable old man in full-on camo. "Because, historically, being a baby didn't always protect you. Think of all those Indian babies who were considered nits."

"Ugh. Colonel Chivington." Segundo suddenly feels sick with history. And sick with the feeling of history returning. Why does Primero always have to remind him?

2

When Jillian first put her hand on the wall of the Casa Blanca, known now as La Casa de los Olvidados, she could feel the building breathing. Until that moment, she'd thought maybe she would paint the outside walls as if to mirror the landscape, brown hills, then green plants, then blue blue sky with white clouds, or maybe she would just paint a fiesta of colors, like a huge firecracker exploding in welcoming celebration. But when she placed her hand there, she knew there was a reason so many walls were whitewashed with lime: this wash was made not only with sand and lime, but also with the mushed pads of the nopal to allow the adobes beneath to breathe. In this way, the moisture the building drew from the earth evaporated back into the atmosphere. The casa blanca, therefore, would always, literally, need to be the casa blanca. It was of the earth and so it needed a porous and breathing skin.

She decided to paint murals on the walls of the inside courtyard where Juana of God used to do her healing ceremonies. This is where the Olvidados and los Viejitos Disorientados—or, as Juana liked to call them in her humorous way, the Demented Elderly—would be spending most of their time. Jillian decided the largest mural would be dedicated to Junie, the channeling Chihuahua. She turned in her notebook to the pages she had sketched that day, so long ago, when she and her mother had brought Aunt Glenda to be healed. Jillian had drawn exactly what she'd seen: the healing spirits emerging from Junie and entering Juana as she performed her miracles.

First Jillian painted a dark green backdrop on which flowers fell or floated. Then she drew the line of supplicants, all dressed in white, their hands crossed over their hearts, eyes closed. Of course, among them, on the far left, was her mother standing next to Aunt Glenda in her wheelchair. Then she drew Juana of God, her white hair braided high on her head, her eyes closed in a trance, her hand held out open, as if to receive an instrument of healing. Beside her, floating in his own trance, Junie. Junie, his tiny body pierced by arrows as if he were a deer in a painting by Frida Kahlo. From Junie the spirits emanated. This had been easy to do in a quick sketch but was the hard part of the mural. The spirits had to be as diaphanous as the gowns in the Botticelli painting Jillian loved, almost translucent, so ethereal that you could see the flowers in the background through them. She wanted to evoke for the Olvidados and Disorientados the flower world that awaits all of us, whether we are ever healed or not.

Of course, Glenda was not the one Juana healed that day. Instead, she went directly to Angie and drew from her stomach seven river stones, big and smooth and black. Jillian's mother was thus cured of her anxieties at least until the twins were born when, in her, born anew, her fear of the power of the world and her helplessness against it. Jillian understood. Motherhood was nothing if not humbling.

The stones that Juana had taken from Angie's body were still planted in the herb garden, which had since become almost as renowned as Juana for healing. Because of these magical herbs, people were still finding their way to Juana's and, in this way, word went out, even en el norte, that Juana was taking care of those who had been forgotten, whether they were the elderly with dementia or soldiers who had been wounded in other deserts on the other side of the world. The Demented Elderly helped Juana in the garden, as best they could, and now there were not only herbs but also tomatoes and chiles and calabazas. The Soldados Heridos helped Jillian gather the nopals for the whitewashing as well as the minerals and plants for the colors on the inside. Those with an artistic bent helped her paint the backgrounds of the mural in the courtyard.

Once the mural in honor of Junie was finished, there were the other walls. Juana decided there should be paintings to honor the saints and she wanted them in the style of the retablos that had been done during the revolution, devotional paintings on tin that could be turned saint-to-the-wall when the Federales came through.

"Oye, Jillian," Juana said, "quiero santos pero..." and she paused, "tú sabes..."

She stood looking at the mural of Junie wherein Junie was much larger than life, as was she, Juana. She went over and touched his image on the wall as if that would bring her closer to him. "Yo no quiero Padre Kino. Ni Jesus. Ni la Virgen," she crossed herself. "Yo quiero santos differentes. Santos de la tierra, del jardin— ¿entiendes?—of the life we live every day."

A ver, Jillian thought. Not being Catholic herself, she had to resort to Google. She found a picture of Saint Jude, the patron saint of lost causes and desperate situations. That seemed to cover most everyone here, she thought, as did St. Anthony of Padua, whose tongue was a relic in the Cathedral in Padua. (The irony of painting him did not escape her.) Plus he was the patron saint of American Indians and their horses, of the oppressed and the poor, of pregnant women and amputees. What a list!

Another irony: St. Juanita was the patron saint of Forgotten People, but no one seemed to know her story. Had it been forgotten? And so what was Jillian supposed to draw around her? Just a bunch of negative space? Or an infinity of question marks? Then she found St. Dude. He wore sunglasses and held a beer and a bong. Patron Saint of Lost Brain Cells. A joke, surely, but why not? St. Juanita, the forgotten saint of those who were forgotten, and St. Dude, the stoned saint of those who were trying to forget.

Jillian tried some preliminary sketches, but her hand was not moving. She decided to take a walk on the red suspension bridge over the dry river and think about it. It was early October. The pilgrims would be coming soon, flooding the town. Maybe she could paint the murals as if they were scenes from telenovelas or horror movies; the saint who had been petitioned would hover in an upper corner, as was the tradition. She had seen retablos in town, for instance, where a woman in a rebozo was being chased through a graveyard by a zombie and another retablo where flames were shooting out of an airplane that had crashed. And another where a naked woman was pole dancing; below her, the faces of the men at the bar, gazing up. Up in the corner, a tiny virgin watching over all and, below the scene, the words: "Virgencita de San Juan de los Lagos, I thank you for my job as a stripper. Thanks to you, I can support my children. And I ask you to protect me in such a tough profession." Jillian supposed there were any number of possibilities for stories of deliverance and salvation.

3

We were in need of a little magic. That's why I took Charlie on the pilgrimage. Nothing for him at the VA. It was all in his head, they said, and of course it was in his head, but the military fucked up his head so why couldn't they fix it? It was one thing after another, first he wasn't eligible, then he was, but no money; then there was money, but not for doctors only for pills; then the price of the pills got jacked and we had to cover them. Besides, just throw fucking pills at him? when the suicide rate of vets is through the roof?—oh, don't get me started.

But it was becoming as clear as day, even to me, that my bitterness was solving nothing. At first, I'd thought, okay, be bitter. Be angry. Look what they've done to your son! You're not supposed to be angry? They use your child as cannon fodder, and you're supposed to be what? Grateful? *I regret that I have but one child to give for my country?* Fuck that. Fuck them. I don't see them giving their children.

And now, here they are, militarizing our own border, militarizing our cities. What the fuck? Black Lives Matter and out come the storm troopers. Poor people running up concrete embankments in Tijuana and we're shooting tear gas at them. Of course, my friends at Pilates all say, "They shoot people in other countries so I don't see why we can't shoot them here." Of course, they shoot people in other countries! Look at my son! They fucking shot at him. Killed his buddy. Bullet went straight through the plate armor. Or think about it, you dumb dildo. They hunt down black kids in the streets almost every day fucking here. No one has to give them permission! Oh my God my anger was making me sick. Time to leave before I killed one of those bitches.

Time to leave. Time to leave. Time to leave. That's what I kept telling myself. Before you have an aneurism or blow something up.

And so we did. We left. We walked with all of the other pilgrims. Only fifty-seven miles from the US border in Nogales. We sold the car there. I've always been good at leaving, at not looking back, and that's what we did. I'd already sold the house and all of our belongings. We kept what we could carry and we walked. The irony of going against traffic—tell me about it! And everyone I knew back home thought I was crazy. The cartels! The cartels! they kept saying, but we walked with all the other pilgrims. How could this be any more dangerous than Iraq, I kept asking myself. Or any more dangerous, for Charlie, than certain streets in St. Louis? Here there were trucks parked by the side of the road and people with water and food. They came out and handed them to us. They wouldn't let me pay. Gifts! In such a poor country! I mean, can you imagine?

We kept walking. It wasn't that hot. Our packs were not heavy. The sky was blue. And open. I started to feel all that anger melting away and, yes, I knew it was a temporary solace. It would come back, it always comes back. I remembered that morning before we left the motel in Nogales. I was blow-drying my hair, round-brushing it. One last time, I thought, and then I'll just let it go frizzy, au naturel, or I'll cut it all off, fucking shave my head, why not?, and I noticed my pulse, just beneath the skin on my wrists. First I noticed it on the right one, then the other. My heartbeat. My beating heart. The thin skin of my wrists. And I thought how easy it would be to end it all. I'd never before seen how close to the surface life was.

And that's what this trip was meant to remind me, I told myself. It's never the destination, it's always the journey. Of course, I knew that, but the journey was short, and the town was this sleepy little Mexican town, very picturesque. I liked all the people in the streets, the musicians, all the shops, the masks of those wrestlers hanging on the walls, the tables filled with plastic saints and religious trinkets. I liked, especially, the deer dancers in the town square, and it was right about then that we saw them: Juana, with her white hair up high in a 60s beehive, and the tall girl with the long hair and cowboy hat. Jillian, we found out. We didn't know who they were at first, although I'd heard Juana of God was a healer, and we didn't realize, of course, until later that Jillian was mute.

Until we saw them, I hadn't known why we'd come, not really, not to Magdalena. Until then, my plan had been to move on after the festival, to keep walking, keep moving south, maybe settle on a beach somewhere. After all, we weren't going *toward* something so much as going *away* from where we'd been.

4

"Sharlie," Juana asked, "Si te llamo Carlos—Carlitos—está bien?" She could tell that his mother wasn't pleased about this renaming of her son, but Carlos it was going to have to be if they were going to stay at the casa for any length of time. They were an odd pair, Juana thought, this white mother and her son who was not white, although what he was, Juana couldn't tell. He had ojos verdes in dark skin. Muy suave, she had to admit. The mother, she had a dragon in her heart, but the son, he was like a hollow bone. All the life had leaked out of him in that desert far away, and the longer he was empty, the more the mother was filling with fire. As it happens in so many families, when one person is out of balance, the others lose balance, too, and you have to bring them back juntos.

"Ya no soy curandera," she told them, "ya no más."

And she took them into the courtyard and showed them the mural that Jillian had painted of Junie helping her heal in the old days. One of the viejitas, Veronica, wandered over and started telling them the story of how Junie had given his life for Primero and

Segundo but, being norteamericanos, they probably thought that this was one of her delusions. Veronica was one of the Demented Elderly deposited at the casa by her family from el norte, but this was not a delusion. It was true.

"La verdad," Juana assured them.

The veil between the living and the dead, between the possible and the fantastic, between what is wise and what is loco, it is so thin, Juana knew, but of course this was exactly what the mother needed to learn. Ademas, it was exactly what scared the son. He had seen people cross over, she could tell, and he had seen them again, after they'd crossed over—something so common and yet, in el norte, strange enough to be the plot of movies.

Since the mother, Gloria, said they wanted to earn their keep, Juana put them to work. She needed help with the olvidados who could not help themselves. This would be good for Gloria since taking care of others is always the best way to heal yourself. Juana assigned Gloria to Veronica, who promptly painted her nails an electric blue and decided they should take a few other viejitas on an outing. Little did Gloria know that Veronica had lost her father and her first husband in two other wars. Someday, this would deepen the bond between them, but right now it was an afternoon of dressing up and going into town for cafecitos y dulces.

Jillian, Juana decided, could use some help on the murals and Carlitos was tall. He could paint the sky. When she went into the courtyard to see how they were doing, Carlitos, who seemed to have a talent for such things, was putting the finishing touches on la virgen in the upper right-hand corner. Beneath her, two luchadores, one in a yellow mask and one in a green, were bathing in an old claw-foot tub together. One was washing the other's back. The other was drinking a beer. Across the bottom of the scene, Jillian was scrawling, "We met in the wrestling and became a couple. We are very happy but don't take our masks off to keep the mystery. We thank the virgin for our big love."

"¡Ay ay ay, traviesa!" Juana started to say, "what am I going to tell el Padre when he comes este domingo?" But then she remembered that Jillian had been sketching the stories of pilgrims she'd met at the Fiestas de Octubre, which is how they'd met Gloria and Carlitos in the first place—and quien sabe, maybe Carlitos had appetites such as these?—so she decided to say nothing. Nada. Any love was good love, pues. Isn't that what the old song said? El Padre would just have to get used to it.

5

Mom, Jillian emailed, *you don't have to sell the house. Just rent it out for now. Just bring Aunt Glenda and the boys. What is keeping you there? We need your help. I want my babies.*

Angie didn't want to say that she was still afraid of Mexico, but she was. Maybe for different—or additional—reasons now. It used to be she was afraid of the cartels. Now she was still afraid of the cartels, but she was also afraid that, when they wanted to come back, the Americans would take the boys away at the border. They would put them in dog kennels. They would make them appear in court to prove their citizenship—after all, they had been born in Mexico— but if any two-year-olds could represent themselves in court, she supposed, it was these two.

And so they made the trek.

"Mamá," Primero cried as soon as he saw his mother. He reached for her with his skinny arms and she scooped him up. He thrust one hand down the front of her blouse, his fingers searching for her nipple, his lips pursing as if he expected to nurse although she had weaned him a year ago. Meanwhile Segundo pressed his face between her thighs as if he wanted to ascend right back up through her vagina into the warm body he'd had such a hard time leaving. "Up! Up!" Jillian nodded to her mother to lift him onto her other hip and there she stood, with both boys clinging to her. The look on her face, it was clear: the separation had been just as hard on her, if not harder.

Angie realized that the three of them would never want to return to the States and if she wanted to be a part of their lives, she would have to quit her job and sell the house. She looked around at the casa, its white walls, the lush gardens fed by the stones Juana had extracted from her body. She looked at the little viejitos and los olvidados, at Nardo and Juana. It was a kind of homecoming, she guessed. She got Glenda's wheelchair out of the trunk and helped her transfer. Maybe this was one place where Glenda could feel useful.

But what is there here for *me*, she wondered. But what was there back home if she left all of them here? If it's true that you have only one life, she thought, why would you spend it far away from those you love most? Still. She wasn't sure she was ready for such a rupture. One life ended, like that! and a new one—not one of her choosing, really—about to begin.

She pushed Glenda into the courtyard where she saw the mural of Junie. There, Juana of God was lifting the black stones from her, from Angie's, own body, something that still mystified her, and holding them in the air as if to bless them. In a way, Angie suddenly understood, those black stones were the foundation of the future, the future for all of them. Okay, she thought. Here. Now. She kissed Jillian on the forehead. She wished she felt like singing.

6

Jillian and Juana had been sitting outside of Jorge's café drinking Bloody Marys and eating tacos de lengua when Gloria and Carlos first approached them. Evidently Gloria had noticed Jillian sketching the pilgrims and hoped she would do their portrait.

"Siéntense, siéntense," Juana had welcomed them, moving her chair closer to Jillian so there would be room for them at the table. "Join us. Pero entienden que this isn't Montmartre. She draws only for herself."

Jillian held up her hand as if to say, okay, it's okay. And then she studied their faces. She drew quickly. But only the mother, her smooth hair, a smooth face, her eyes expectant, because this is what Jillian knew the mother would want: her thirty-years-younger self, herself as she wished to be, all possibilities still in front of her, none of this knowledge that life can change in a way you never wanted. None of this sorrow. Jillian ripped the drawing out of the sketchpad and handed it to her.

"Oh, but I wanted one of us together," the mother said.

"Pues, sí," Juana said. "That would have been ideal."

Jillian had already sketched Carlos when she first noticed him in the crowd of pilgrims. She had sketched him in his greenish underwater world, although it wasn't underwater, exactly. It was moonlit and starlit with shadows moving through the soupy green, skinny beams of light shooting back and forth, bubbles of light trailing in an arc through the sky, and then big lasers from shadows in the sky. Explosions of light led to explosions of darkness. Then a shower of fireflies.

Why green? she wondered. She looked at Carlos. His food had come, and he was hunched over it. No one is going to take it away from you, she thought, and then she heard the words, *electrons, clouds of electrons, they excite the phosphors. Which are painted on a screen.*

When she looked down at her drawing, she heard other words. *Go go go go. Roger that.* Swearing, of course. And then there were other sounds, the rapid zinging of automatic weapons, the percussion of explosions, but they were a kind of background noise for the voices because, she supposed, she was hearing his thoughts, his memories, and in them, the sounds of the weapons receded but the voices stayed. Some were simply human voices in languages she couldn't understand. Some were animal sounds made by human-animals, the language of fear or pain or dying that needs no translation.

But it was hard to hear anything more than that, what with the noise of the fiesta all around them and with Juana explaining to Gloria about the casa: "The demented elderly and the head-injured young, those are our—¿como se dice?—niche markets—if I want to think in the way of los norteamericanos. Where everything is bottom lines. Pero, what is my bottom line, I asked myself el otro día. Who would most benefit from la casa? Y ya lo sabía: those who can never be healed, but who want to live with freedom. Tú sabes. As if their minds are still whole."

Jillian closed her eyes and decided to put her hand on Carlos. After all, what could happen? He was already a shadow of himself. He could shrug himself further away, if that was even possible. He could stand and leave. But he didn't. She could feel that her own fingers were cool when they touched his arm and they warmed up as his memories started seeping out. Whispers of Carlos, the memories in his muscles, the things he had buried inside. *No egress,* she heard, and then, *enfilade.* She saw doorways in a line. Enfilade. As in to thread a needle? From the French? She waited. *No. As in a volley, as in a volley of gunfire, a valley of gunfire. Along a line. From end to end. Gunfire, from end to end. Enfilade enfilade enfilade. No egress.* He'd been trapped. He was still trapped. He had lost people. They had not wanted to leave this earth but at the moment they did, all their love and all their grief had soaked into him. She felt their electricity passing from him to her and, eventually, she knew, she would release it into the paintings on the walls of the casa where, finally, it could be breathed out into the air.

7

Primero and Segundo, like all two-year-olds, ran full throttle, albeit somewhat unsteadily, from room to room in the casa, and from courtyard to garden and back. They were like tiny drunken adults. Or, maybe, like teenagers on acid, their hold on reality that tenuous. They picked up crayons and said, "Color? Color?" They were mesmerized by Juana's jewelry. "Earrings?" They longed to put anything shiny or delicious into their mouths. They wanted to consume it all, even their mother, their kisses open-mouthed as if they could devour her.

They were happy at the casa. Because their mother was busy painting and their nana busy helping Juana do her niche marketing on the slow-as-molasses internet, they spent most of their days with Glenda and the Demented Elderly. First thing, after breakfast, they ran out into the gardens ahead of Glenda in her chair. She had to sit at the end of a row, say, while they weeded with their little plastic rakes or sprinkled water out of a can. The Demented Elderly helped supervise, which, of course, they loved to do.

"Right up their alley," as Primero liked to say.

But he and Segundo were accomplished at ignoring their elders, so no problemo, and the calabasas y los melones grew so big and so heavy that it took two of the demented ones to carry them to Glenda in her chair so she could wheel them into the kitchen. And so it went. Tomatoes, red and ripe and juicy, and when sliced, one slice would cover a dinner plate.

"Biblical," Segundo would say.

"Like the loaves and fishes," Primero agreed.

"Like water into milk," Glenda said.

"A miracle, for sure," all the Demented Elderly agreed, "water into milk."

Since their own synapses frequently misfired, they just left it at that and, although it didn't sound quite right, water into milk was just what the casa was going to need for all the babies who were massing at the border and who would be, unless there was a tectonic shift en el norte, turned away.

"Because," Segundo said, "no more welcoming the stranger."

"No shit," Primero agreed, "although there's plenty of scripture that says, basically, Open the Fucking Door."

"OMG!" Segundo mocked his brother. "Primero! You sound like Nana!"

"Make the table longer, that's all I'm saying."

And with this, they couldn't help but remember the long table that had stretched across the border on the day of their birth, how it had been full of revelers who looked up from their meal to see their mom, heavy with them and stumbling down the side of the canyon. The revelers had gone to her aid without hesitation or debate and carried her to open doors on this side. Had it not been for them, Primero and Segundo knew, they would have perished with their mother in that canyon of looming boulders.

"We would have been eaten by coyotes," Primero said quietly.

But Segundo was remembering how Juana of God had to reach up and pull him out by his ankles. At least he would have died safe inside his mother, he thought, and not lonely and exposed on a hillside.

8

The trickle of refugees had been small at first. Of course, it had been happening for years. "So many," Juana told Angie as they sat in the courtyard one morning with Nardo, drinking their coffee. "So many." And when had it started? She tried to remember. Long before Junie died.

"It was because of La Bestia," she said. "La Bestia runs on its tracks not so far from here, pues, and when someone falls off and an arm or a leg is caught beneath its wheels, los otros hop off the train and stop the bleeding. They carry the mutilated ones—¡ay, pobrecitos!—sometimes it is so bad you don't even want to remember— they carry them into Magdalena where they hear about me. Juana of God. And then they hope so much! Pero, por supuesto, not even I can make limbs grow back."

"Not even when you had Junie's help," Angie said. "Of course not."

"Nadie puede hacer tal cosa," Nardo nodded, "but, Juana, other healing takes place. Healing, it is muy misterioso." He looked at Angie. "As you know. And no one is ever turned away."

But what were they going to do now, Angie wondered, and so did Juana and so did Nardo. The refugees were no longer a trickle, not a few unfortunates who had been maimed under the wheels of a train. No. Whole families, a caravan of people, parents and their children, Angie had seen them when she brought Glenda and the boys south. Juana had been sending Nardo and los desorientados into town every day with stacks of corn tortillas and whatever other food they could spare. But now, the refugees, having been turned away at the border, were coming to the casa, a casa that was already full and already consuming everything it was able to produce.

"What about those you've helped over the years?" Angie asked. "Have you kept in touch? Maybe they would donate? Or let's think of churches in the US. Or maybe you could go on Oprah again! Maybe we could become a foundation."

"Give us your olvidados, your desorientados, your soldados heridos; give us your masses yearning to be free," Nardo said.

"¿Por qué no?" Angie laughed. "That will be our motto. Our mission statement."

"¿Por qué no?" Juana echoed. "There's got to be a niche market. ¿No? Los que quieren justicia para todos? ¿Como se dice? The woke?"

"Oh, Juana," Angie said. "Yes, the woke. We'll preach to the converted."

She opened her laptop. Did she believe in the power of the word? That was the question. But what else could she do? Tending one's own garden was not enough. She had once thought it was and that it was, realistically, *all* you could do in such a complicated and conflicted world. *Candide*, of course. But was Voltaire being ironic? It was a luxury to tend to your own garden. That's what it was. A luxury. Of the privileged few. And she'd never realized it.

9

Jillian did not want to be drawn to Carlos. After all, she already had Primero and Segundo and her mother to love, not to mention Glenda and Juana, and she was very busy painting the murals—she painted like other people breathed—but there was something about his biceps. She wondered why the arms of men, when they were muscled just so, were achingly beautiful. And his chest and the line of his jaw and his skin, just a few shades darker than her own, and the line of his neck as it became his shoulder, and the line of his neck just below his ear where she longed to place her face at night and breathe. And the muscles of his stomach, the line of hair just below his belly button, her hand could not help but stray in that direction, her palm flat against his belly, her fingers inching their way below his waistband. Oh. And that was what she wanted and what she wanted, she wanted.

And wasn't wanting enough? That was what she wanted to ask him as she crawled into his bed at night, after she got the boys to sleep in their crib. She would crawl into his bed and stretch out alongside him. Pressing into his side with her whole body, she could suddenly feel her breasts, her nipples, her pelvic bone, her clit, that warmth that woke every cell in her body, that electric warmth, she pressed harder, she wanted more. She nuzzled his neck, her mouth open against his warm skin, her hand moving over his chest and down. He never said no. Instead, he turned to her or pulled her on top of him, his hand knotting her hair on the nape of her neck, and then they were kissing, kissing as if it were breathing, and then, sometimes, he was above her or, sometimes, she was above him. Still later, her thumbs tracing his eyebrows and then his lips and he would run just his fingertips up and down her back, giving her chill bumps. His eyes. She would always remember his eyes.

Juana was right: he was very good at painting the sky. Sometimes, when they were painting, if no one else was there and sometimes, even if someone else was there but they weren't watching, she would press herself against him, her front against his back, her arms around him and run her hands up under his shirt, against his bare chest. To tease him. To remind him. She liked it when he laughed.

But there were other times, like when she had to leave his bed in the middle of sleep, because one of the boys woke up or because she had to pee, she knew not to get back in. It could be dangerous to surprise him. And she could tell there were times when it was better not to get into his bed at all. Not even to knock at his door, and instead, to leave him locked in his own darkness.

Days were sometimes serious, too, and then he asked her to drive him all the way to the border, all along the border, just on this side. He wanted her to show him the canyon where she had been lost with the boys and almost perished and the Women's Collective where the boys had been born. He wanted to see where there were breaks in the wall, where there was no wall, where there was only a barbed-wire cattle fence, where the border was still an invisible line on the ground. He wanted her to teach him the desert and so she did. She walked before him on the trails on both sides, she led him through arroyos and canyons. She showed him paths that people and animals had been following for thousands of years. She showed him where water might pool, where it might be hidden, where provisions might be stashed. She showed him the evidence of those who had passed this way before them and of those who had been left behind and of those who had died. She showed him evidence of destruction and malice, the slashed water bottles, the cans of beans which had been left by the Samaritans punctured by others and left to rot.

After that, when Jillian woke in the night, his space in the bed was often empty. If one of the boys needed her, she would bring him back with her, but if she had wakened and both boys were still asleep, she would find herself restless with vigilance and so, often, she would go out to the courtyard and light candles. In the half-light she would begin to draw. She used charcoal, her hand moving quickly across the rough stucco of the walls. Dark, shadowy scenes would emerge. In them, a moon, clouds, maybe the clouds would fall into a canyon. Shadows of people beneath trees, hiding behind boulders, carrying children. She felt as she had when she'd drawn maps for the migrants she'd found in the desert, as if she were giving them a possible future. Here is water, a field with food, a car with gas and a kind driver, a train slow enough for you to hop aboard yet quick enough for you to flee. Here is a Border Patrol lookout; here is a ranch where the owner carries a rifle and has been known to use it; here is where smugglers hide out, waiting for the weary. Here is a place to rest, a person who might give you water or food or money or sanctuary. Here is the way to your new home where relatives and friends are waiting. Here is an angel or an ancestor to watch over you.

In the mornings, when Carlos and the other soldados emerged from their rooms, they appeared to be fully rested, and Jillian wondered if she had dreamed Carlos's absence. In fact, sometimes, when she awoke, he was lying in their bed, the boys between them. On those days, she felt slightly disoriented as they ate breakfast, as she and Carlos went to work painting the murals and the others left to work in the fields or to care for the children. Maybe it was sleep deprivation, she told herself, but weren't there always new faces at the table? More babies for the Demented Elderly to feed? More lost children and grieving parents hoping to find one another? She watched as Juanita counted the mouths. She never seemed surprised. She just put extra pots on the stove for extra beans. She just assigned the grieving adults to tortilla or garden or baby duty.

Also, in the mornings, the charcoal sketches on the walls had often been transformed into scenes, some in full color. Jillian wasn't always sure how that had happened, either, although she would awaken with dabs of paint on her hands and beneath her nails. Some of the scenes were of people stealing through the desert, children in their arms, but others were scenes like those in bark paintings of entire villages. The people were like limbs on a tree of life, roosters crowing the sun up, gardens vibrant with plants, fish swimming in pools of clear water. Abundance. She was painting abundance. *And, here, Carlos, is the way back to our bed.* This, she scratched into each drawing, under each painting as if it were her signature. A petition to saints she wasn't sure were listening.

10

We dreamed communally in those days and, in a mysterious way, were apprised of the news before it ever hit the papers or airwaves or even the internet. We knew about the seven-year-old Guatemalan girl who had died of dehydration in the custody of the Border Patrol, for instance. We dreamed of her spirit haunting the desert and of her mother's spirit searching for her. La Llorona took on a new meaning for us: all over Mexico and Central America, they were crying, the mothers, for their children. And, yes, we heard that the girl had been sick when the Border Patrol found her, but we also knew they had waited eight hours before giving her medical care. We hoped, then, that the ghosts would rise in vengeance. Really. We hoped that. We dreamed it. And we, the Demented Elderly, we were not a vengeful people, but there was being borne in us a hatred not only for those who hated but also for the heartless and even for the merely indifferent.

The babies, Primero and Segundo, they dreamed of these things, too, we were sure, because when they awakened in the middle of the night, their cries were frantic. Sometimes we heard them even before they cried and certainly before Jillian heard them. We would be lying in our own beds, awakened by our own dreams, where, over and over, there was a cement embankment and we had to run up it, babies in our arms, children hanging on to our clothing. We were all tired and thirsty and hot and dirty. We ran toward the rusted iron slats of the wall and, because the wall was slatted, we could see through to the other side. There we saw another wall, but one that was impenetrable, made of the bodies of men in uniforms, men with helmets and machine guns, men who were being paid to act as if they were only bodies, no hearts or minds of their own. Behind them, we could see people kneeling in the dirt or kneeling in the water. Sometimes they were in the tides. Their hands held out, palms up. The men would bark at them and beat them back and, sometimes, arrest them, dragging them to the drab vans that would swallow them.

And then they would shoot the tear gas through the wall at us. We noticed, then, that the slats were the color of dried blood. There was a reason for this, we thought; even in our dreams, we were aware of their motives. We were trying to hold the children and protect their lungs from the gas and still run with them, back down the embankment. Of course, we fell. We could feel the hard cement against our knees, the rough texture, how it tore at our skin. The children we were holding were ripped from our arms or sometimes we would drop them in the stampede for safety and we knew we would never find them again. Such was our sorrow in our dreams that our sobbing would wake us.

And this is how we knew the twins were dreaming what we were dreaming. They woke up wailing and sputtering and choking. They could not breathe. Their knees and elbows were scraped, as were ours. It was as if what was happening to others was leaving its mark on our bodies.

Of course, had we not fallen back into our own bodies, we would have felt nothing. Most of us had felt nothing for years, it seemed. We'd been numb. But after Primero and Segundo came to the casa, we started to fall back into ourselves again. There is no other way to describe it. Holding them and comforting them reminded us of the years we'd held our own children. Primero often looped his arms around our necks, just as our own daughters might have done, and Segundo, apropos of nothing we could see, would run to one of us and rub his face against our thighs. Such tenderness bloomed in our chests at those moments! We felt young, hips wide, breasts full, arms open. The children had no sense that our bodies had become husks, shells, and so because of them, we began to come alive again—but, as we all know, being alive has its own consequences.

Some days, and it could happen while we were lying on the floor doing yoga, we would spread our arms and close our eyes, perhaps for prone spinal twist, and suddenly we could feel ourselves falling back, say on the grass as a girl, or falling back on a sandy beach, or back on a bed, husband then, or lover, suddenly above us, young, too, or not so young. We said their names, we said their names aloud, we told them we loved them. We called them to us, our longing so strong we willed them into existence. We kept our eyes closed and felt the weight, the heat of their bodies through the veil. In such a way, our spirits and our minds became stronger and, because the spirit and mind need a body to live in, our bodies became stronger, too, and more capable. And, believe us, we had known even then that it would take an army of viejitas to take care of all of the lost children.

First, we dreamed Carlos into action. Yes, as unbelievable as it may seem, this is what happened. In our dreams, we began to see him leave the grounds of the casa in the middle of the night. He was going on a kind of reconnaissance, we guessed, looking for los niños perdidos or their wounded and weeping parents. Gradually other Soldados Heridos went with him. They were sweeping through the desert between here and the States, even into the States. Some said there were raids on stash houses where smugglers kept their human cargo. Some said there were raids on the detention centers where 15,000 children were being held and made to sleep in cages as if they were animals. Some of the children, Carlos and the others led to safety in el norte. Some they brought here, of course, and we noticed the numbers tattooed on their forearms. The trickle turned to a river and we had to clean and rebuild the old orphanage where Juana of God had grown up as a child. We, the Demented Elderly, liked to call the orphanage the Casa Annex, as if we had forgotten its real name but this was because none of us wanted to say, over and over again, La Casa de los Niños Perdidos. We did not want the children to be lost. We wanted to hold them in our arms and feed them and watch them grow fat and sassy. We wanted their parents to come and find them.

And all the while Jillian painted. Oh, how she painted. All of our dreams and all of our lives adorned the walls, first of the casa and then of the orphanage. Which came first? The dream or the life? We didn't know.

11

And here, Carlos, is the way back to our bed. But, of course, one night he did not return. There were conflicting stories about what had happened. Some of the soldados said that they had been leading a few deported parents back to the states to look for their children when they were surrounded by men with automatic weapons, possibly drug smugglers or coyotes who thought they were in their territory. Others were sure they were already in el norte and the men were ranchers or Border Patrol. True, there was a lot of shouting in Spanish, which increased their confusion, but some cited the bright lights shining in their eyes as evidence. The way they were handcuffed and made to sit in a row. The way they were taken one by one into the darkness, away from the others, to be interrogated. No way that was some damn coyote, one of them said. But they all agreed that it was in this moment of chaos that Carlos had disappeared. Had he vanished of his own volition? Disappeared into the desert? Or was he disappeared into one of the trucks and taken away? They didn't know. They knew only that when the men with weapons took the deported ones away and they were left standing in the darkness, Carlos was not among them.

When he didn't find his way back after a few days, Jillian and a few of the soldados—those without head injuries because it was hard enough to remember where you'd been without short-term memory loss—decided to retrace the journey of that night. Of course, this journey took days, weeks, even, instead of hours because in every village, every ranch, every colonia, la gente wanted to know about Carlos and they wanted to tell his stories—how he had led someone they knew to safety, restored a child to a family, reunited family members, how he and the soldados had repaired roofs or walls or roads or brought water to a field full of dying corn because, of course, most of the villages were empty of men. Jillian wondered when he'd had the time to do all of this, but it was clear his presence had become mythic. Everyone was sure he could have defeated any and all foes, whether ranchers, smugglers, coyotes, Border Patrol, or even Federales, such was his cunning and his strength.

When Jillian returned from this journey, she drew the homes they had visited, some of them made of cement blocks, some of shipping pallets or aluminum or even cardboard. The roofs, corrugated tin. The floors were the earth swept bare and tamped down with sprinkles of water until it was as hard and shiny as tile. Blankets hung in doorways. Windows? Not always. Electricity? Running water? Sewer? No. Cooking was done inside over small improvised stoves and so the children were wracked with coughing from the wood smoke. If there was water, it was kept in metal drums from the maquiladoras, drums that had previously held chemicals and now held a murky soup teeming with larvae and other tiny creatures.

Jillian tried to draw all of this, but stark realism was not in her artistic repertoire and she struggled. Van Gogh's *The Potato Eaters*, Goya's *cuadros negros*, Käthe Kollwitz, Siquieros, these were her influences: she had a whole wall of stark experimentation, all done in charcoals or very dark colors, her anguish there for everyone to see.

But she wondered what the point was, if her paintings changed nothing. If children still lived in such abysmal conditions? And in worse conditions than simple poverty, worse when you added in the violence of the cartels. She drew boys as young as ten being conscripted as sicarios, mothers digging holes in their yards where they could hide their daughters. Some days she could barely bring herself to work. She felt she was merely documenting. There was no vision. There was no joy in the act of creating, nothing imaginative or transformative, nothing that would ignite the world. It began to feel like therapy, which embarrassed her. Was she grieving that much over Carlos?

12

Angie had always thought that Jillian was a visionary, even when she was little and was painting those weird Boschian scenes where men had grapes for heads. True, she thought, as she looked at the latest murals, they weren't the scenes of deliverance and gratitude that Juana had wanted but maybe they were just as important. She took Juana into the courtyard and pointed at the homes that needed repairs, the crops withering in the fields. "Maybe we should start sending the soldados out to help," she said.

"A ver." Juana looked worried. "We'll have a hard time if we give away their labor," she hesitated, "pero, podría ser, que si la gente tiene sus propios jardines..."

"We could raise more money on the website?" Angie suggested.

That very night, Angie could have sworn, the Demented Elderly dreamed that Carlos had, in fact, been taken by the Border Patrol and was charged with a felony for harboring migrants. In their dreams, they said, he was known as Charlie-Carlos and they watched videos of him giving food and water and clean clothing to two men, videos that the feds planned on using in a court of law against him! They woke up incensed. "He was charged with federal crimes," they announced at breakfast, "for humanitarian aid! For giving people water and food! Humanitarian aid is legal! Yet he's facing twenty years in prison!"

This lit a fire under Gloria who had been holding her breath. She and the demented ones searched all the news stations and the internet. Nothing anywhere. Not in English, not in Spanish. It seemed, in these dark times, that some news was invented, and some disappeared as quickly as human beings and their bodies did.

What to do? They had no choice but to act on the available intel from the demented ones' dreams. The viejitas made signs that said, "Free Charlie-Carlos!" and "No More Deaths!" and "Humanitarian Aid is Legal!" Jillian helped the children dip their hands in buckets of bright paint and decorate the signs with their handprints. Gloria told Juana she was going to rent a bus in Magdalena, one of the nice passenger ones, and fill it with los soldados y los desorientados y las viejitas, whoever wanted to go and had the proper papers. They planned to drive to Tucson, which had the nearest federal court.

Juana was a little nervous about this. The Demented Elderly, especially las viejitas, were her bread and butter, after all, and so, even though she'd been reluctant to do so, she finally called Oprah on her special hotline. Oprah had made no secret of the fact that she thought El Chillon was un Chillon grandote and a gilipollas to boot, so she did a special show about Charlie-Carlos and the other soldados heridos and all the work they'd done in the countryside helping the poor even though they, themselves, had little money and had been screwed over by the VA. Oprah's crew filmed all of Jillian's murals, too, sometimes as background and sometimes up close, and as they filmed the unfinished ones, Angie told the story of Jillian's painter's-block.

The program was a tear-jerker on so many counts: parents making pleas to be reunited with their children, lost babies in the laps of las viejitas, the other forgotten and demented ones working in the gardens or the kitchen or cleaning the buildings and grounds, and los soldados heridos, abandoned by the very government that had sent them to war. And, of course, Oprah had not yet heard about Junie's death and how he had given his life to channel the spirits so that Jillian's babies could be born. Juana of God was standing in front of Junie's mural when she told Oprah, unrehearsed, on the air, cameras rolling, this dramatic story. Juana began to cry, as she always did when she told of the self-sacrifice of her dear one, and Oprah, hearing the story for the first time, broke down, as any person with a heart would do, and the ratings went through the roof. There had to be a sequel!

Because everyone in el norte would like for their demented elderly or their brain-injured young to become celebrities, it was now no risk to Juana for Gloria to rent the bus. Oprah's crew filmed everything. Los soldados, los olvidados, los desorientados, and the army of las viejitas with their electric blue fingernails filing on the bus: how they sang songs all the way across the border, how they chained themselves together outside of the Federal Courthouse in

Tucson and waved their colorful signs aloft while chanting No More
Deaths! No More Deaths! No More Deaths! The demented ones
had had accurate dreams and so it came to pass that they chained
themselves for two weeks before Charlie-Carlos's trial, to ramp up
publicity, as well as on the very first day and so, as he was being led,
in shackles, into the court house he saw them, all of his beloved soldados y olvidados and, of course, his faithful mother.

13

Later, when Jillian was old, it would not surprise her that she felt
such nostalgia for these years. After all, even though the boys were
becoming more independent, she still spent hours feeding them,
changing them, bathing with them, her skin against theirs as she
washed and dried them, her hand ruffling their hair dry so it would
curl. How many hours were still spent lifting them, kissing their
round cheeks, holding them on her lap as they ate, in her arms as
they fell into sleep, sleeping with them curled against her?

It was hard to pay such attention to the body without being acutely
aware that this closeness was fleeting and without being reminded
that the veil between life and death was thin. So thin. One slip in the
bath, one fall down stairs, one illness, one high fever. She was constantly aware of their whereabouts, constantly listening for and to
them, even for and to their breathing, her consciousness and theirs
so permeable that she knew they felt her anxiety about leaving them
with her mother so she could join the olvidados to protest in Tucson.

She had already been separated from them, of course, more than
once, and that had been hard enough, but she'd known that she
could go back or that her mother would bring them to her. Now the
situation at the border was so much worse. If the Americans knew
she was part of the protest, what would they do? Or what if they or
the Mexicans prevented her from reentering Mexico afterwards?
And then, worst of all, what if, when her mother tried to bring the

boys to her in el norte, they were taken away at the border and put into those cages?

She knew her fears were dark and wild, illogical. No one is going to take your children away, she told herself. You look white, you're a citizen, privileged. But because she knew the full weight of their physical presence, she also felt the full weight of possible absence, an absence that would have been not only like empty arms but amputation, each child a ghost limb.

Still, she was trying to be rational. She steeled herself. The boys would be safe with her mother and Glenda. They had been safe with them before. She needed to see Carlos, to reassure herself that he was still alive. If only she could see him, she knew a map for his return would flow from her fingers. Plus, she missed him. Of course, she missed him. She wondered if he would be allowed to hold her. If they would be allowed to touch one another at all. She longed to touch him. To hear his voice. To exchange a look.

She packed and unpacked her bag several times. Three pairs clean underwear, a bra, a few toiletries, period supplies, just in case, a pair of jeans, two clean blouses, a sweater for the air conditioning of the courthouse where she planned on drawing the proceedings. She packed her sketchpad and favorite pens. But every time she was ready to zip the bag closed, she felt sick to her stomach. She made herself lie on the bed and breathe: you don't have to go, she'd tell herself, nothing says you have to go, nothing says that your going will change a thing, nothing you do will change his sentence or bring him home earlier.

Finally, because she had given herself permission to stay, she decided to go. She zipped the bag and walked out to the bus where everyone was waiting for her. From Glenda's lap, Segundo waved, "Come back? Mamá come back?" At this, Primero cried, "Mamá!" Once. And then threw himself headlong out of the wheelchair. When Jillian picked him up to stop him from banging his head on the ground, as he did when he was feeling especially adamant and helpless, his fear shot into her veins like an electrical surge. She saw the bus crashing, she saw gang members stopping the bus and boarding it, she saw the soldiers at the border boarding it—Federales this side, Border Patrol that. Their guns, their boots, their helmets, their masks. She saw herself in chains, in jail, not able to get back. She saw the casa burning, her mother trying to save both boys but not strong enough to carry them, not strong enough to run with them from the cartels who would surely come because, after all, the money flooding in from Oprah's show was a double-edged sword. The casa now had something they wanted. She saw the boys conscripted into their army of sicarios, even though they were so young, *because* they were so young, their brains malleable, the fact that they would be safe from prosecution. She saw the older sicarios rip the food from their mouths, bully them, turn them against each other. Primero and Segundo! Against each other! Expected to have a higher loyalty to the cartel than to one another. And how could she protect them from el otro lado, from el norte?—but how could she protect them from *this* side? How could she protect them at all? She felt all the fears rise up, inchoate, and grip her heart. She felt Primero's arms, so thin, flung around her neck and tightening, and Segundo, who had climbed down out of the wheel chair, trying to climb up her legs. He was braying like a little mule. His tears were real.

She stood there with both boys. She didn't even have a chance to write Carlos a letter. Gloria said, "Don't worry. I understand." A little too breezily, perhaps, Jillian thought. She watched Gloria climb up the stairs and into the bus; she watched as the doors pneumatically shut and the bus left without her.

14

This is what Charlie-Carlos said on the witness stand: "When I look at them, I see bones. The person in the flesh, I see their bones, and then I know they won't make it unless I help them."

What he didn't say, even as he looked out on the people in the courtroom, was that he could tell who was at risk of perishing soon, for whatever reason. Cancer. Heart attack. Car accident. The ordinary ways of dying.

At this very moment, down in Magdalena, Jillian was drawing the bones of an eight-year-old girl dissolving into sand. It had been 108 degrees the day she died of heat stroke, her mother having left her behind to find water. There were bodies everywhere, Jillian knew this. Not bodies. Sets of human remains. That's what they called them.

Charlie-Carlos had seen eighty-eight sets, he told the prosecutor, eighty-eight, and when he saw the bones, there on the desert floor, exposed, sometimes scattered by animals, he couldn't help but feel their alone-ness.

This is why they called to him, he speculated, because he had seen bones in the war, too. And because he had been in the war and because he'd done things that required atonement, when he saw the bones inside the flesh of the still-living, he knew he had to act.

"It isn't, really, a matter of choice," he said.

"Besides," he reminded the prosecutor, "Humanitarian aid is not illegal."

Down in Magdalena, as Jillian painted the bones of the eight-year-old girl, she couldn't help but think of Primero and Segundo, how close they had come to the same fate, there in the canyon on the day of their birth, how, if Nardo hadn't sent his cousins to help her, her boys' bones—and hers, too—would still be there. She shivered. Even at midday, she shivered, the ghost of her near-death passing by and, at night, when she tucked the boys into bed and kissed their foreheads, she couldn't help but feel their skulls under their skin, how smooth the skin, how thin the bone, how slight the distance between here and there.

"The jig is up," the prosecutor said to Charlie-Carlos, his voice full of gravitas. "The jig is up!"

"The jig is *up*?"

This voice was Gloria's. She was seated in the courtroom, surrounded by the Demented Elderly. She shot out of her seat. Verily, she was vibrating.

"*The jig is up?!*"

Beneath her skin and flesh, her bones began glowing, and so Charlie-Carlos blurted out, "*Mom!*" And not because he was afraid, as he had been as a teenager, that she was going to make a spectacle of herself, but because he was afraid she was going to have a heart attack or a stroke or an aneurism. Or something.

"*What the fuck does that even mean?!*" Gloria wanted to know.

"Tell them, Charlie," she said, "tell them that our policy, US policy, has been one of systemic violence for decades. We have pushed migrants more and more into the regions that are not habitable, not crossable, not endurable. Where there is no water. Where temperatures are 112 degrees for days on end. Where the temperature on the surface of the earth can reach 180 degrees. Where their tongues swell and turn black. Where their brains boil in their skulls. Where, in their delirium, they try to drink sand."

The Demented Elderly started snapping their fingers.

A ripple went through the courtroom.

Even the Bible, which the Demented Elderly did not necessarily believe was the Word of God, said to treat the stranger, the sojourner, as a brother. "*For I was hungry,*" they began to chant, "*and you gave me food, I was thirsty, and you gave me drink, I was a stranger and you welcomed me.*"

Etc.

Jillian, in Magdalena, tried not to think about Charlie-Carlos in the courtroom, facing twenty years in prison for providing water and food and medical assistance, something the people in the town of Ajo had been doing for generations. She knew, of course, that they wanted to make an example of him. They wanted to send a message. They thought they could kill compassion. They thought if people died, others would stop coming, but all over Mexico, women were searching for their missing children. The Colectivo Solecito had excavated 250 skulls near the city of Vera Cruz alone, she'd heard, and they'd found 3,900 bodies across the country—3,900 desaparecidos found, out of 37,000. She began to paint a huge mural: the courtroom, Charlie-Carlos on the stand, the prosecutor pacing, Gloria and the Demented Elderly. Then, below that scene, the women of the Colectivo hammering a length of rebar into the ground at a suspected gravesite, the stench of death emerging, the digging, the skulls, the waiting for the results of DNA tests. Then another scene, women protesters with green bandanas across their faces dousing the policia with pink glitter, their banners unfurling on the diagonal: No me cuidan. Me violan. They kill us and you do nothing.

"Tell them, Charlie," Gloria continued, for no court of law was ever going to silence her, not when the life of her child was at stake and, truth be told, Gloria had always worried only about her own child, his education, his opportunities, his well-being. She had never worried about the children of others until it was too late, until his life depended on the children of others, until she saw him devastated by the sacrifice—needless, in his opinion—of the children of others. "Tell them, Charlie, remind them. Our fingerprints are all over the Northern Triangle. Remind them of our complicity in the overthrow of democratic governments, in the coups, in the massacres, in the disappearances, in the death squads, in the torture..."

The Demented Elderly were standing now. They were snapping their fingers again. The judge began to drum his gavel on the bench, but it didn't silence anyone. In fact, it only emphasized the rhythm of their chanting, providing punctuation after each mention of the sojourner: "*You shall not oppress a sojourner. You know the heart of a sojourner, for you were sojourners in the land of Egypt.*"

"Not to mention," Gloria continued, ignoring the judge, ignoring, in fact, everything around her except for the sight of her son on the witness stand. "Not to mention," she continued, "our hunger for drugs, our lax gun laws. And what about inherited trauma? And what about the detention centers?"

At this, the Demented Elderly closest to Gloria could feel the heat emanating from her skin. They would swear, later, that they could see the sparks in her eyes, the way her hair was rising from her head as if electrified.

One of the Demented Elderly, he was nearly one hundred, and blind, stood and the chanting stopped. The sound of fingers snapping, that stopped. Even the judge ceased with his pummeling of the bench.

"We died," the old man said softly, "of the conditions. We died from being crowded into barracks where there was no room to sleep. We died from not having adequate nutrition and from a lack of hygiene. We died because, although our clothing was washed, the temperatures were not hot enough to kill the lice. We died from typhus spread by the lice."

Jillian, even down in Magdalena, had heard about the camps. She had heard that there were 929 people living in a space meant for 230. She had heard there was no room to sleep. She had heard they were not allowed to bathe, were not given soap or water or clean clothing. She had heard about the stench of so many unwashed bodies crowded into too small a space. She had heard about the lice and it made her skin crawl, her scalp. She had heard they did not have clean water to drink, that they were denied vaccinations and medical care, that children had been taking care of babies, that children had been dying.

But she could not draw this, not while it was happening. Something in her was superstitious. Something in her wanted to document it as a part of the past, not as on-going. Something in her wanted only to distance herself from the unimaginable. She wanted to hold her own children and kiss their sweaty heads and wash their grubby hands and faces and think of it as simply ordinary, an ordinary chore, and not a blessing bestowed upon her simply because of the fortune of her birth.

In Tucson, the judge resumed with his gavel and two guards began to make their way toward Gloria through the crowded courtroom. The Demented Elderly linked their arms. The frail one, the old man who had spoken, stepped in front of the guards, shielding her.

"I am going to give my testimony," she shouted. "I was here the last two Tuesdays when the migrants were brought in, seventy at a time, shackled together, for mass hearings. You can hear the shackles, the chains, before you see them, the men, the women, in the same clothes they were wearing when they were detained in the desert. This is a culture of cruelty! This has been a culture of cruelty! 30,000 instances of abuse by the Border Patrol in the past three years. Not giving water. Not giving medical care. Sexual assault. And now this is being visited on *children*, in *our* names, and you call it a *jig*..."

And then, mid-paragraph, Gloria burst into flames.

Some say it was a magic trick. After all, as soon as the pandemonium in the courtroom stopped, as soon as the fire extinguishers had finished extinguishing the fire, there was no trace of Gloria. There was no pile of burnt clothing, no burnt body, no smell of a burnt body, not even a pile of ashes. But also, there was no trace of her son. Charlie-Carlos had disappeared. And if it weren't a trick, wouldn't he have leapt from the stand and tried to save his mother, hero that he was?

But those standing closest to Gloria, the Demented Elderly whose clothing and hair were singed, insist it was spontaneous combustion and the fact that Charlie-Carlos had also disappeared was merely a part of what they perceived as divine intervention. Not a trick at all, but the miracle they'd all been hoping for.

15

Jillian is lying on her bed. She can hear both boys breathing. She longs for Carlos, it is true. She has never longed for anything or anyone more than she longs for him in this moment. She closes her eyes. The sky is the blue of winter. There is wind. She feels her hair fanned out around her. She feels her skin against the gauzy cotton of her nightgown. She feels the air press against her face. She feels Carlos near her. He whispers and she feels the heat of his breath as it enters her ear. She sees the map that will bring him home. She can see it and she can see, suddenly, little Junie with his bug eyes. He has come with an image for a painting; it is a vision about how the world might be made whole. There are flames. There is water. There are sheaves of green corn. There are women standing, holding hands. They are wearing green bandanas and saris and rebozos and gymnasts' outfits and other colorful clothing. Their arms are crossed in front of them; they link their hands. She can smell the fragrance of their hair. She can smell the flower world. She opens her eyes and Carlos is there, in the flesh, next to her in bed. His breath is on her neck, entering her ear. And Junie is there, still there, floating above her in a bubble, tongues of light surrounding him. He is no longer pierced by arrows.

Acknowledgments

I have so many people I would like to thank for helping me with this book. Barbara Cully, Fernando Alvarado, Alicia Alvarado, Irene Cooper, and Brigitte Lewis, who listened to me read drafts aloud. Susan Roberts, Karen Brennan, Aidan Coryell, Esme Schwall Weigand, Kindall Gray, and Boyer Rickel for reading. Pam Uschuk, Frankie Rollins, Ru Freeman, and Melanie Bishop for their support. Kathryn and the twins for inspiration and for reminding me of what really matters. Michael, Justin, Sara, Jax, Gavin, and Ollie for giving me a home. Junie for channeling the spirits even after he was gone.

I want to thank Diane Goettel at Black Lawrence Press for her expertise in editing and in all phases of publication and promotion. I want to thank everyone at Black Lawrence—what a challenge and labor of love to produce such fine books in such trying times. Thank you to Jennifer Tseng for cheering me on once the manuscript was finished; to Kimi Victoria Eisele for her beautiful cover art; to Rosalie Morales Kearns for her expertise and help in promoting the book; to Andrea Hopkins for proofreading all of the Spanish. Finally, my gratitude to Oregon Literary Arts for awarding me the 2020 Oregon Literary Career Fellowship.

Finally, I would like to thank the following editors and journals for publishing individual stories and excerpts from stories: *The Southern Review, Terrain.org, Western Humanities Review, Atticus*

Review, Cleaver, Shirley, Lunate, About Place Journal, Eleven Eleven, and *The Drunken Boat: Librotraficante Issue.* I would also like to thank Rosalie Morales Kearns for including "Dear Juana of God" in the Shade Mountain Press anthology, *The Female Complaint: Tales of Unruly Women.*

Photo: Hannah O'Leary

Beth Alvarado is the author of three previous books: *Anxious Attachments* (Autumn House Press, 2019), *Anthropologies: A Family Memoir* (University of Iowa Press, 2011), and *Not a Matter of Love and other stories* (Winner, Many Voices Prize, New Rivers Press, 2006). *Anxious Attachments* is a finalist for the 2020 Oregon Book Awards and was long-listed for the PEN America Diamonstein-Spielvogel Art of the Essay Award. For much of her life, Beth lived in Tucson where she taught for the University of Arizona; she now lives in Bend, Oregon, where she is core faculty at OSU-Cascades Low Residency MFA Program. She is on the editorial board of *Puro Chicanx: Writers of the 21st Century* sponsored by *Cutthroat: A Journal of the Arts* and the Black Earth Institute. Her essays and stories have been published in many fine journals including *The Sun, The Southern Review, Guernica: An International Journal of Politics and Art,* and *Ploughshares*. Individual essays and stories have often been nominated for Pushcart Prizes and three essays have been chosen as Notable in *Best American Essays*. Beth won an Oregon Literary Career Fellowship.